WOLF

Also by Martin Bell

The Way of the Wolf

Return of the Wolf

Night Places

Distant Fire

WOLF

MARTIN BELL

A BALLANTINE/EPIPHANY BOOK

BALLANTINE BOOKS · NEW YORK

A Ballantine/Epiphany Book
Published by Ballantine Books

Library of Congress Cataloging-in-Publication Data
Bell, Martin, 1937–
  Wolf.
  "A Ballantine/Epiphany book."
  1. Christian fiction, American. I. Title.
PS3552.E5179W65 1989   813'.54   87-47501
ISBN: 0-345-33773-5

Text design by Holly Johnson
Manufactured in the United States of America

First Edition: January 1989
10 9 8 7 6 5 4 3 2

For Mark and Randy

"You know what I'd like to be?" I said. . . . "You know that song 'If a body catch a body comin' through the rye'? I'd like—"

"It's 'If a body meet a body coming through the rye'!" old Phoebe said. "It's a poem. By Robert Burns."

"I know it's a poem by Robert Burns."

She was right, though. It is "If a body meet a body coming through the rye." I didn't know it then, though.

"I thought it was 'If a body catch a body,'" I said. "Anyway, I keep picturing all these little kids playing some game in this big field of rye and all. Thousands of little kids, and nobody's around—nobody big, I mean— except me. And I'm standing on the edge of some crazy cliff. What I have to do, I have to catch everybody if they start to go over the cliff—I mean if they're running and they don't look where they're going I have to come out from somewhere and catch them. That's all I'd do all day. I'd just be the catcher in the rye and all. I know it's crazy, but that's the only thing I'd really like to be. I know it's crazy."

—J. D. Salinger
The Catcher in the Rye

CONTENTS

WOLF

CONRAD

1

Doggone that little train. It shoulda been right there in the window. It should. Paw says maybe come Christmas. Maybe Christmas, he says; only now it ain't there no more. So how's Santa supposed to know where it's gone?

My shadow is behind me, walking on the windows of the stores when I pass.

Across the street, hearing the street and the traffic, I can see them—the people idle in open doors. It is almost Thanksgiving. Terry Lee and I are going to cook chicken for Paw on Thanksgiving.

And I can feel it in my throat, but I can't stop it. Because my eyes are already burning with it, and I am running beside the wall now. Doggone that train. Doggone it anyway. How's Santa supposed to ever know? I am clutching at the sides of my trousers as I run. The trousers are too long; I haven't had time to grow into them.

Then I come to the park. All around, through the trees, the afternoon is slanting. He is sitting on a folding chair, kind of humming and playing his guitar. He looks at me. "You folks want to hear me sing a song?" he says. His guitar case is open on the ground beside him. In it are quarters and dimes and a crumpled dollar bill. There is a big old dog sleeping next to the guitar case.

Upon the cold air, chimes come, sounding above the downtown streets and buildings and trees. I sit on a bench, with my legs in the sun. Then he is singing. "For your wishes, for your heart's desires," is what he sings while I listen and listen and the dog's ears keep twitching.

I am thinking, They taken it out of the store window, so how can Santa? How can he?

Sitting on the bench, thinking, hearing the music a long time, I can feel my own breath on my face and see the cut place on my finger where it doesn't hurt anymore. Then I hear the running and I quit thinking and turn around and see her coming along the sidewalk, running. Terry Lee is my sister. I wave my hand to her because she is still looking at distance, not noticing me. There is snow in the air.

Terry Lee stops running and looks at me.

"What is it, Terry Lee?" I say.

"Where have you been?" she says. "It's late. Where have you been?"

"I went to see it," I say, "only it wasn't there."

"What do you mean?"

"That little train in the window. They taken it away."

"Oh, Conrad," she says. Like that: Oh, Conrad.

4

And then she says, "I swear, sometimes my heart feels like it must surely break."

"Why, Terry Lee?" I say. "Why does sometimes your heart feel like it must surely break?"

"Come on," she says, "let's go. Paw's putting supper on and we're late."

While we walk I can still hear him, who sings about wishes, about the heart's desires. But he is not singing. He is talking. "How about it?" he says. "You folks want to hear me sing another song?"

2

After supper Paw pushes his chair back from the table. He says he's got choir practice tonight and it'll be late when he gets home.

I clear the table. Terry Lee washes dishes, and I wipe—only not put away because I can't reach.

Paw sings a little. He is in the bedroom, getting ready. Terry Lee and I aren't going to play checkers while he is at the choir. We are going to play cards.

"Look there," I say, "your fingers are all wrinkled like prunes. Your hands too."

"It's from the dishwater," Terry Lee says.

We are going to play cards later.

"Terry Lee?"

"What?"

"How come Paw sings at the Congregational Church, not at our church?"

"Because the Congregational is a paid choir and ours ain't."

Terry Lee is my sister. She does not go to the same school as me; she is in high school.

"Paw gets paid for singing, ain't that right?"

"That's right."

From the bedroom he emerges. His hair is wet and combed; it smells like lilacs. He has on his Sunday pants. "How do I look?" he says.

"You look fine, Paw," Terry Lee says.

"Now don't wait up for me," he says.

"All right, Paw," we both say.

Then he leaves.

Terry Lee doesn't look at me. She stands sort of quiet for a minute in the lilac smell, while I am thinking about the little train and Santa and Paw's deep voice singing in the choir on Christmas.

"Terry Lee?"

"What?"

"Is it wrong for Paw to get paid for singing in the Congregational choir?"

"No. Of course not. Wherever did you get such a strange idea?"

"Billy Roberts says our minister told his ma."

"What? Told her what?"

"Told her that Paw should sing at his own church for a change, instead of always thinking about money."

"Let me tell you something," Terry Lee says. "Mrs. Roberts ain't never known poor. And neither has that dumb old minister, I reckon. You remember that, Conrad."

It's because me and her were born so many years apart, and already she is in high school—that's how she knows.

"Terry Lee," I say, "are we poor?"

"Go on and get them playing cards," she says.

"All right," I say.

I get the cards and we play rummy. We play for a long time, with Terry Lee helping me to make books and to figure my score.

Some folks has big, pretty houses; others hasn't even an upstairs apartment, like we do, to stay in.

So I wonder.

Across from me, quiet and thin on the couch, Terry Lee sits playing cards. I can hear the whistling sound when she breathes; she is breathing with the thin whistling sound that is her asthma. Ma always used to say it ain't nothing to worry about; she said there wasn't nothing wrong with Terry Lee that moving back up north wouldn't cure. To remember the northwoods with, to help her breathe better when the asthma gets bad, Ma gave her this little pine-smelling pillow with on it crocheted a green little pine tree.

"You want me to read you a story?" Terry Lee says.

"Yes," I say.

7

She is gathering up the playing cards now, closing them away in the box. She looks at me. "What do you want to hear?" she says.

" 'Rumpelstiltskin,' " I say. Then I say, "Terry Lee?" but she is already getting the book, so I go in the bathroom and put on my nightshirt.

Twice she reads "Rumpelstiltskin." I know it by heart and I say all the words inside while she is reading. I lie on the couch with my blanket and my pillow and my stuffed bear. Terry Lee sits in Paw's chair where she can see if I am asleep yet.

"Go to sleep, Conrad," she says.

"All right," I say.

Then, while I am lying with my eyes half-shut, she closes the book, turns the light off, and goes into her room. I hear her a long time breathing in the room. Then it is dark everywhere and I can feel myself floating, drifting sort of. Terry Lee is still my sister and I am still me, even though everywhere it is floating now, drifting, going on the track around and around until finally it isn't floating anymore; it isn't anything anymore, and I am asleep.

3

"You, Conrad!" Billy Roberts yells across the schoolyard when I am starting to leave with my quarter. "Conrad! Wait up, will ya! Where ya going? Can I come?"

"No," I say, walking.

Without turning around, I wave my hand for him to go back. The street is louder and louder ahead. I walk fast up the street on the narrow sidewalk, stepping on my shadow, hiding my face from the wind with the collar of my coat.

Then I look back. He is behind me.

"This ain't the way home," he says, hurrying, nearly running.

"I know," I say.

"Where are we going?"

"Billy," I say, "why are you following me?"

"Following?" he says. "You?" he says.

I walk faster, not looking back. The road goes between unpainted houses with broken fences and everywhere weeds growing in the yards. It does not occur to me that he might not be there, might not be in the park with that big old dog lying on the ground next to him. All I can think of is those folks putting money in his guitar case, like it was some kind of special wishing well, and him singing about wishes too.

Out of breath, puffing and puffing, Billy Roberts says, "We're going downtown. Ain't we, Conrad? Huh, Conrad?" He walks beside me now. "Downtown," he says.

We reach a traffic light and cross a busy street where the jumbled, shabby stores begin. "Hadn't you better go on home, Billy?" I say. The sidewalk is of concrete—broken, cold with late November.

"I don't have to mind you," Billy says. He gives me a look, screwing up his face.

Then we are walking beside the wall, not running, but walking pretty fast. We go on. We go to the park, where pencils of afternoon sun slant through the trees. Two women sit on a bench, talking and smoking. I can see things like whirling glinting things spraying across the sunlight behind them. In my hand the quarter is tight-held, secret. But nowhere do I see the man or the dog or the wishing case—the guitar case where folks put their money.

"What?" Billy Roberts says. "What is it?"

Then I hear the chimes, crisp and distinct and sad, spaced along the cold November sky. And I am thinking, Where is he? Where is he? while all around, the sound of the chimes is dying away into trees. Thinking, Doggone that little train. Doggone it anyway.

4

It is the last day of school before Christmas vacation when the teacher says, "Conrad, your father is here to see you."

"What?" I say, not understanding.

"Out in the hall," she says, "your father is waiting."

"Here at school?" I say. "Paw?"

She takes my hand and walks with me out into the hall, where I see him. He looks tired, with on his face a kind of sad, wrung-out expression. His voice, downcast, says, "Conrad, something has happened to Terry Lee. I need for you to come home now," his voice says it while his eyes keep moving from side to side.

"What is it, Paw?" I say. "What has happened?"

He is standing there before me, in the hall, with his tired eyes not looking at me, with on his face that expression both empty and waiting. He has already got my coat from the coatroom.

I know what this is like, I think, thinking, This is like it was when Ma was dying. "Paw," I say, "is Terry Lee sick? Is it her asthma? Is that it?" All the time I am watching his lowered face, the awkwardness, the hurt.

"No," he says, "not asthma." He says in a faint, blurred voice: "Some boys . . . bad boys . . . beat her up. At school this morning they did. Some wicked, wicked boys."

It does not make sense to me.

"Why, Paw?" I say. "Why did they?"

"Here," Paw says, in that near whisper, as he is putting my coat on me, fumbling, trying to make the zipper work; only it's broken, so he can't get it to go right.

11

Suddenly I am shivering, not with cold. I say, "Terry Lee is going to be all right, isn't she?"

He does not answer.

"Paw?" I say.

"God willing," he says, "she's going to be just fine."

Then there is silence again. And together we walk through the halls. Outside, everything looks sort of white and frozen and still. Beyond the schoolyard I can see the roofs of all the houses where clouds of smoke are rising from chimneys without any wind.

5

While I am sitting near the couch, with my coloring book open on my lap, I talk to Terry Lee. Her face is worn and pale, her eyes quiet and dim above the covers. She just lies there, holding to the quilt. I talk to her about how this is Christmas vacation and tell her what I am coloring and ask does she want to play rummy yet.

"Do you want to play rummy?" I say.

Terry Lee does not say anything. She does not look at me either.

"That's all right," I say. "You go ahead and rest some. Me and you can play cards later."

At night now Paw keeps the lamp by the couch lighted; in the daytime too; it makes Terry Lee feel some better. Ever since it happened, Paw comes home to fix lunch every day, fixing hot soup for her so she will be sure to eat. Only still I wonder. I wonder why did they. But Paw says he doesn't know what to tell me, so I don't ask about it anymore.

Christmas is three days. It shouldn't mean nothing that the little train ain't there in the window; it shouldn't mean Santa can't find it.

I tell Terry Lee that Christmas is three days; does she want me to make her a list for Santa today, or wait until tomorrow when Paw brings home the tree? I tell her how the little train is all I am wishing for, and how I keep on wondering if Santa really can.

Then it looks like she wants to sleep, because she closes her eyes and turns her face to the couch.

"I'll be quiet now," I say, "so you can sleep."

After which I color more in my book, coloring careful and slow while inside of me I tell the story I know by heart—the one about Rumpelstiltskin.

Then I hear a strange, choking sound coming from where Terry Lee has turned her face to the couch. Her shoulders are shaking, and she is wheezing when she draws in a breath. At first I am frightened. But then I realize what is happening, and I say, "It ain't no need to cry. Everything will be all right. It ain't no need to cry, Terry Lee."

The lighted lamp stands on the floor beside the couch, with on it a fluted shade of biscuit-colored plastic shading the bulb. The apartment is quiet. Once in a while a car passes in the street beneath the window. And I am thinking, Around and around all shiny and bright on the track it goes, clattering on the little steel track around and around.

6

Walking fast, my collar turned up, I walk by the storefronts and the coughing men with red eyelids and then along the wall to the place where the park begins. I start to run just before I reach where he is and I see him.

He sits erect on the folding chair, leaning forward a little, his guitar held tight against his body. On the ground nearby, the large dog is full awake, watching.

I lean against a tree, listening to him, hearing him pick with his fingers the steel strings of the guitar. After a time I can't hear anything except the words of the song, those same words again, "For your wishes, for your heart's desires."

My shadow, on the ground beside me, is as still as the shadow of the tree, but I can feel my heart going fast, thudding in my voice. "I got a quarter," I say, loud. "I got a quarter for the wishing case." In my clenched hand I can feel the hard edge of the coin.

While I walk toward him, flecks of sunlight dapple everywhere. On the folding chair he waits, smiling, not looking at me. I put the quarter in the guitar case and say, "Here it is," taking two long steps back. He sits on the chair, smiling at the trees, his lean face all alive and calm and waiting.

"It's Christmas tomorrow," he says. "You folks want me to sing a Christmas song?"

"Yes," I say.

"All right," he says.

Then I, sitting on the bench with flecks of sunlight dappling and dappling around me, hear him begin to sing. In a hushed, clear voice he sings, "Silent night, holy night. All is calm, all is bright." That is when I make my special wish. I shut my eyes and, with my eyes shut tight, I wish for it until my head hurts with the wishing. It is because tonight is Christmas Eve and the tree and the lights and Santa too.

Now his voice is mellower, clearer than before, singing, "Sleep in heavenly peace," while I am thinking, It's Christmas Eve and she ain't made a list yet. All this time and Terry Lee ain't even made a list for Santa. She just lies on the couch at home, wrapped in that quilt, still not saying anything to me, or to Paw either.

Yesterday when we put up the tree, Paw said I should be sure to turn the Christmas lights on tonight for her to look at. Because until ten or ten-

15

thirty he will be at church with the choir. I am staying up late this year, maybe to see Santa even.

That is what I am thinking when the song ends, when the man says, "Thank you. Thank you." He says it to the air, sort of, and bows, like there were lots of people standing around. "Thank you," he says.

I don't know why, but all of a sudden I get mad at our minister for saying Paw should sing at his own church, instead of always thinking about money—as if that's the only reason Paw sings. In the park it is still like there were lots of people standing around, with him bowing and saying, "Thank you. Thank you." So I decide maybe I have missed someone, and I look to see who else is there.

But it ain't no one else there besides me.

7

There are lights on the tree, and ornaments. On the soft-needled branches of the white pine, the Christmas lights wink and tremble.

"Oughtn't we to turn off the lamp now?" I say to Terry Lee. "So it will be more like Christmas?"

Her eyes watch me. It is as if she is deciding something, trying to say something.

"What do you think?" I say.

CONRAD

She turns her head away, holding to the quilt. I cannot see her face anymore.

"Tonight is Christmas Eve," I say, "and Santa. Is that what you are thinking about, Terry Lee? Is it?"

From beyond the dark window comes the sound of a car passing slow along the street. And I am humming, Silent night, Silent night, as I walk over to the lamp and put my hand on the switch. "I'll turn it off now," I say. "Is that all right?"

She does not answer.

"All right?" I say.

Still she does not answer.

So I turn off the lamp. And immediately the room is filled with Christmas, reflecting from the tree all red and silver and gold. I sit on the floor. Looking, I can see Terry Lee has turned her head a little to watch the lights; her eyes are full open.

Then she says, "Conrad, listen to me. Santa's not going to be able to bring you the little train." Her voice is kind of dry, whispery-like—but she is talking, Terry Lee is finally talking. "He is very sorry," she says. And she says, "I am sorry too, Conrad. I really, really am," while she opens and closes her eyes in which the tree lights are swimming now like tiny flames.

"It's all right," I say. "I already know. I know the train ain't coming." I say the words while I am smiling and smiling, watching Terry Lee's face, thinking, Thank you, thank you, as the tiny flames flicker and swirl, while the tiny flames flicker and swirl in her eyes. It is because of him who was in the park and the big old dog too, because of. Only Terry Lee doesn't know what I asked for in my special wish, so she worries about the little train.

"You needn't to worry, Terry Lee," I say.

"Oh, Conrad," she says. Like that: Oh, Conrad. But before she can say anything else, I have an idea; I go and get the cards for us to play rummy.

She says, "Do you want to play rummy?"

"Yes," I say.

I hand her the playing cards.

"All right," she says.

Then it all flows together in the room—what I am feeling and the undimmed lights of the tree and the sense of Santa in the air—while I am smiling and smiling, saying, "I've got a secret, Terry Lee."

"Do you?" she says. Her eyes are round, bright.

"Yes, I do," I say.

"Conrad," she says.

"What?" I say.

"Merry Christmas," she says.

And then me and her play cards until Paw gets home.

A LAMENT

In the springtime of our repentance,
  we cannot shake loose of the world.
Through mazes of temptation we walk,
    feeding on the sweet fruit of power, ignoring the
      cries of hungry children.
Separation among us deepens,
  and cords of death encompass the earth.
Progress cannot bring salvation;
  neither can the past heal the wounds of today.
Give ear to our prayer, O God;
  in our distress we call upon you,
    the rock of our salvation.

Under the shadow of Babel,
  we play upon instruments that are out of tune.
Beneath hanging gardens in the city of no-hope,
  we sing as a people divided,
      a nation of dry bones.
Behold the wilderness around us;
  behold the land of ashes and exile.
Earth is convulsed with death;
  the land is polluted with blood.

WOLF

We have corrupted the house of the Lord,
  making of it a smooth thing,
    a tower of protection from the lion of Judah,
  and from the snarling of God's wrath.

We say to God, our rock: Have you forgotten us?
  Weeping, we remember the land of promise,
    the glad shouts and the songs of thanksgiving.
Why do you hide your face, O Holy One?
  And why are you so far removed from us?
The way is dark and slippery;
  we are as children who do not know how to go
    forward or back.
Restore us, O God;
  let your face shine, that we might be saved.

Hearken to me, my people whom I have called;
  I will yet give health to you
    and heal your wounds
  and relieve your shoulders of the burden.
From afar will I save you;
  and bring your children out of the land
    of their captivity.
Because I have loved you with an everlasting love;
  therefore shall I continue in faithfulness to you.
The sun will not set on the promise of my covenant;
  nor will darkness prevail
    against my eternal Word, says the Holy
    One.

A LAMENT

Glory to the Creator, and to the Redeemer,
    and to the Sustainer of all:
as it was in the beginning, is now,
    and will be for ever. Amen.

REBA

Moving quietly, she enters the vast, sleepy kitchen. Blue enamel pots steam dry on the long, polished, wooden counter. The kitchen is nightshadowed, dark. Now, more than eighteen years familiar, she walks across the halfseeing with an air of steadfast confidence, gliding almost, or so it might seem to another watching.

The house is quiet but not asleep. She knows that beyond the moist hot dark, the children are not sleeping. Yet she does not bother about it because no one is crying and because she believes that she knows better than to look in on them when they are quite sleepy and a little out of sorts and maybe just that close to being full awake.

In nearly all ways the corridor from the kitchen to the parlor reminds her of a church. Brass chandeliers—three of them—sprout from the high ceiling like so many sheaves of gold lilies. Sometimes when she passes beneath the chandeliers, she walks slow with her hands pressed together, like a monk in a monastery. She thinks then about the hollow, noisy wards of the hospital where the children were for so many years, thinking, *How can I carry it? How can I?* though perhaps it was in one of those deco-

23

rous, peaceful moments also that she thought for the first time, *It will be all right.*

Now she passes under the chandeliers. Her glance goes to each of three carved doorways along the corridor; it is as if she can almost see the breathing that her ears can hear beyond those doors. But she does not pause. Three rooms; six children: Their faces rest on the surface of her mind, light and transparent as the skin on a pond. *I will carry it,* she thinks, continuing toward the front hall, *I will carry it and it will be all right.*

Her thick-soled shoes strike with faint thuds the slate floor of the entranceway. She delays before securing the front door, hesitates before turning the heavy deadbolt, staring at the door's leaded glass windows, listening. But it is her own blood she hears, not footsteps on the ancient porch, not a hand lifting the doorknocker.

"No one is missing," she says to the cloudy, rough squares of glass. "Every one of them has come home," she says. And her voice keeps a peculiar rhythm as if the words are being sung to the music of some forgotten song. At last she throws the deadbolt, moves away from the door, and enters the shadowfilled, moonlighted parlor.

It is past midnight.

But Reba is not thinking about the time or the shadows or the swollen heat. She crosses the parlor. Before sitting down she takes the unopened Bible from its place on the table and lays it on the arm of her large chair. It is not leatherbound, not expensive; it waits there, insistent. But she does not open it yet. She sits down. She sits without haste in the large chair; then she turns slightly and snaps on the lamp. Across her lap cuts a thin shaft of light from the shaded reading lamp sitting on an end table. She takes from the chair arm the Bible and opens it between her hands. For a moment she merely looks at the page, seeming not to comprehend what it is that she sees. Then her mouth gives shape to the words, ceaseless, silent, one following another like raindrops on a glass pane.

Night has not yet cleared the parlor when Reba wakes. Looking down at her is a man with curly brown hair, a grown man who is dressed in corduroy pants and a red shirt.

"Tommy," she says, "what are you doing up and dressed?"

"Ain't doing nothing," he says. And he smiles.

"You got powdered sugar on your mouth," she says. "You been eating doughnuts."

"No," he says, still smiling, looking at her. "I leave 'em be."

"Oh, Tommy," she says. "You didn't leave them be. You went and ate the Sunday doughnuts."

Shaking his head, he says, "I never." Then he says, "How come your face looks stepped on?"

Reba closes the Bible, places it on the end table.

She switches off the lamp. "Slept on," she says. Early morning gray enfolds her and Tommy and the furniture shapes. "It's because I fell asleep in the chair last night. That is why my face looks that way."

"How come did you?" Tommy says.

"Now don't go changing the subject," she says. "You are just changing the subject away from the doughnuts."

Tommy moves to one side as Reba stands up. He is taller than she. He says, "I hoped it. I hoped we could talk about something else."

"Uh huh," she says. "You hoped it would all go away. Only that's not the way life is, is it? We are talking about the doughnuts because it is what happened."

"I wanted 'em," Tommy says.

"Well," she says, "I reckon there's nothing to be done about it now. Do you remember how many are left?"

For the first time Tommy's eyes leave her face. He seems to be reading the complex topography of the room. "I don't know . . . a lot . . . some . . . I can't remember."

"Is anyone else up?" she says.

"Up?" he says. "Only me and Merle. He is also eating doughnuts."

Reba moves down the hall past the bedrooms toward the kitchen, which is filled with a warm coffee smell. Entering, she sees him where he is sitting at an enormous, round, oak table. The shallow, white bakery box is nearly empty of doughnuts; powdered sugar covers the entire table. On the wooden counter the percolator sounds a loud, liquid cadence. "Merle," she says, "those are the Sunday doughnuts."

"I know," he says. "For today."

"No," she says. "Not for today. Today is Saturday. Sunday is tomorrow, Merle."

"Oh," he says. He looks at his powdery fingers.

"It will be all right," she says, going to the sink, wetting a washcloth. She hands the cloth to Merle. "You and Tommy clean up the table; I will make breakfast."

For a while the three of them work without speaking. Then Tommy says: "Do you go to the bakery today, Reba?"

"Yes," she says. "I work at the bakery every day except Sundays."

"Can you get more doughnuts?" Tommy asks. Sugar clings to his red shirt; he looks tired.

On the stove is bubbling a pan of white gravy; mounds of biscuit dough wait on the kneading board. "Maybe," Reba says. "I hope so. But you know what I have said before: The woman who owns the bakery always takes the leftover doughnuts from Saturday to her church on Sunday. She lets me take the leftovers on Friday night."

Merle and Tommy say, "Oh," at the same time. Their faces are confused, sad. Merle says, "I forgot."

"Never you mind," she says. "What's done is done. Besides, you made us all some coffee, didn't you?"

Merle nods. "It's my job," he says. "In the morning I make the coffee."

"That's right," she says. "Making the coffee is your job. And you did it just fine." She kneads and cuts the biscuit dough, singing to herself. It is a hymn that she sings, ever stronger and stronger until she is singing full out the words about Jesus and the Rock and the River Jordan. Her bones do not hurt so much now. And after a while she says: "Tommy, you can call the others to breakfast. The biscuits are almost done."

By seven o'clock Reba arrives at the small bakery where she has worked for nearly ten years. The shop is located on the main street of town; next door to it stands a small cafe with red leather booths, and across the street is a jewelry store. Many of the other stores at that end of Main Street have already moved to the shopping centers. It makes Reba sad to see the empty windows with in them all those curling, faded For Rent signs; they look so sullen, so dead.

But she is not thinking about the empty shop windows this morning as she waits on the children and the grown-ups who line up in front of the wonderful bakery display cases. Saturdays are especially busy for Reba; she is almost as busy on Saturdays as she was years ago when customers used to crowd into the shop every day of the week. Like a priest preparing the sacrament, she moves in an unhurried fashion among the shelves, packaging each order, tying twine around white cardboard boxes. It delights her to dispense the cakes, cookies, and bread, even though by noon her feet are aching and her right hip has begun to twinge with pain.

At 12:15 P.M. Reba stops working and says, "Excuse me for a moment, please," more to the air than to anyone in the bakery. She walks a little awkwardly, a little carefully, to the back room where is her lunch of a cup of coffee and a piece of cornbread; nothing more. She eats. Yet she does not rest. She can still see the shop, the display cases, the customers. Her face is watchful; it is the face of a store manager. And when the cowbell that hangs on the front door makes its familiar, hollow, clapping sound, she looks at the two women who are entering.

The women, whose names Reba cannot remember, enter the shop and remain standing by the door; they converse in hushed tones. Whenever these two come in the bakery, they keep a little island of silence about them, whispering, laughing. Reba imagines they are talking about her, gossiping about the dark house where she and her children live; speaking of the disgrace of it, shaking their heads about those grown imbeciles; isn't that what they say: imbeciles, retards, feebs? In her rage, in her impotence, Reba imagines they are talking about the children.

And the longer the women wait near the door, the more she herself wants to say something. It occurs to her that there may well come a time when she will speak of it to them, telling aloud of how so many people with their whispering and fears have harmed the children. But for now, she says nothing; the words remain enclosed, locked within a shadowed region of her mind. In truth, she knows she will never actually speak out. She knows it because if she were to raise her voice against those who resent the children, if she were to do that, the hospital would tell her they could no longer approve her home for care of the mentally retarded: not if she causes trouble; not if any of the children causes trouble. *No trouble*, she thinks as she packages a dozen raspberry turnovers for the women who wait before her, *No trouble, for sure*.

"Will there be something else?" Reba says.

"No, thank you," one of the women says in a level voice that is now in motion, going away. Then they have left the shop; the cowbell claps loud behind them.

When Mr. Simmons arrives, Reba knows it is three o'clock. He comes to the bakery precisely at three o'clock every day Monday through Saturday, the days the jewelry store across the street is open. Facing him across the clean glass counter, Reba first pours a cup of coffee, then selects a large cinnamon roll, which she hands to him. "One cinnamon roll," she says.

"Someday I'm gonna surprise you, Reba," he says. "Someday I'm gonna ask for a glazed doughnut."

"No, you ain't," she says. "You are flat addicted to those cinnamon rolls, that's what."

He says, "Wait and see. I can stop any time I want to. Maybe I just haven't wanted to yet." He bites into the roll. Then he asks her about the children and especially about Robert.

Reba looks away. "Why, Robert is fine, Mr. Simmons. Just fine. It is absolutely his pride and joy to be learning to read and write. And he is doing very well." She says this so that the actual truth might be told, yet told in a way that will avoid the jeweler's being disappointed. But as Reba speaks, she is remembering the struggle, the anger, the tears; she is thinking of how Robert has, after many years, only learned to read and write his name: practicing over and over again, forming the letters, persisting. Aloud she says, "Robert tells me that just as soon as he learns to write, he is going to write you a letter."

"Well now," Mr. Simmons says, smiling a little, looking down at his coffee. "Well now, is that a fact?"

Around them, everywhere, are warm pastry

smells. Reba shifts her weight off the bad hip and turns her head until she can clearly see the doughnut rack. *They went fast today,* she thinks; *of a certainty there won't be enough leftovers for me to take home; I know it.*

Mr. Simmons finishes the cinnamon roll. But he does not leave. He acts as though he is about to say something, something that cannot easily be put into words. His shoulders are stooped from the work of engraving silver; he reminds Reba of a drawing in a book she once saw: It was a picture of an old woodsman with secret, magic powers. For a time she watches Mr. Simmons who does not move, does not speak. Then, at last, he puts some money on the counter and says, "I figure that should be enough to cover the coffee and the roll; am I right?"

"Just right, Mr. Simmons," she says as she does every afternoon, Monday through Saturday. The cowbell makes its clapping sound again, the screen door bangs, and Mr. Simmons is gone. Slowly Reba looks out toward the street, watching as automobiles slide past the bakery, their hoods reflecting the weary, midafternoon sun.

By the time the owner of the bakery, who is Evelyn Garner, comes to get the leftover doughnuts and take the day's receipts to the bank, the clock says quarter after five. By now Reba is sweeping and dusting and rubbing fingerprints off the glass-fronted cases; to herself she hums a nameless, steady tune, one which she has made up from parts of other songs.

"A pretty good day, yes?" Mrs. Garner stands behind the cash register, not looking up. The wiry old woman, who baked every day for more than forty years, working until her hands finally went bad with arthritis, and who, even now, daily collects the cash receipts and also advises Reba and the others, says, "It was a pretty good day."

"Yes," Reba says, "today was a good day," as she watches Mrs. Garner assemble two white bakery boxes and pack into them all of the leftover cookies and doughnuts. The air hangs suspended, motionless, in the small shop. Reba clears her throat.

"What?" Mrs. Garner says. "What is it?"

"The leftovers," Reba says. "I was thinking maybe I could buy some of them from you."

The older woman raises her eyebrows. "So? But what about Friday's? Didn't you get Friday's leftovers?"

"Mrs. Garner," Reba says, her face suddenly hot with lying, "to tell you the truth . . . I dropped them, all of them." *It is not right to lie*, she tells herself, *but God will forgive it; God will*. For a brief moment the two women look at each other.

Then Mrs. Garner says: "Oh, Reba, I'm sorry; I truly am. But I can't. I just can't spare any of these. Tomorrow we're having Brother Ellard, that visiting preacher; remember I told you? If it was any other time, you know, any other time. But not now; not with Brother Ellard coming. I'm sure you understand." Then the bent fingers close the shallow white boxes and stack them, one on top of the other; it is a gesture of finality.

"Of course," Reba says. "Of course I understand, Mrs. Garner." And she resumes cleaning.

Placing the cash bag in her purse, picking up the white boxes, Evelyn Garner says: "By the way, how are those young men of yours getting on? Is everything OK with them?"

Reba says, "Getting on fine, Mrs. Garner." As she speaks, she is hearing the children's voices asking about the Sunday doughnuts, while she is thinking, *It is not my fault; they will just have to remember to count the days. It is not my fault.* Yet her troubled heart will not be comforted and she continues fretting the matter, saying aloud to Mrs. Garner, "Getting on just fine. I will tell them you asked after them."

Now in the changing light that is reflected by the glass-fronted display case Reba sees the faces of Tommy and Robert and Merle and the others. Their disappointment is so vivid, so palpable, that it blocks the sound of the cowbell and Mrs. Garner's goodbye. In a soft, indomitable voice, she speaks to them, soothes them. "Never you mind," she says. "It will be all right. There is something special about people like us. God made us to be special."

———

REBA

She locks the bakery shop door and moves slowly away from the Saturday afternoon emptiness of Main Street. When, at the end of the block, she turns a corner into the western sky, the lowering sun hits her eyes, and a headache needles the skin of her forehead. She walks on, leaning hard against the heat and the sudden light.

Leaning, Reba knows this: On the way home she will pass the factory where are baked all the commercial breads and pastries—a bloodless factory that is filled with noise and unending conveyor belts. To think of it makes her angry. People buy factory bread because it is easier to get than fresh baked; at least that is what customers tell her when they are standing in Mrs. Garner's shop, explaining why they come only on special occasions to the bakery and no longer place orders for the week ahead. "There's no holding back progress," they say, and Reba, walking slowly along the hot pavement, shakes her head at the memory. To her it does not make sense. She cannot recall ever having seen anyone smile when touching or smelling a loaf of factory-made bread. *But I reckon they have their reward*, she thinks. *And I reckon they call it progress.*

Near the factory stands a small thrift store where day-old baked goods are sold. Reba stops in front of the store, staring at the boxes of prepackaged doughnuts that have been placed in the display window; she is still worrying about Merle and Tommy, worrying too about what the others will say when they learn there is no Sunday treat. *I will tell them I was not able to get any. I will tell them I am too old to be baking late on Saturday night—that's all there is to it,* she thinks. Downlooking, she moves forward again, walking more swiftly. But then the bad hip catches her, and she nearly cries aloud with the pain.

For a moment she pauses, watching as cars flow out of the factory parking lot. It is quitting time. And absolutely no one notices her standing there. Traffic bunches at the exit; several drivers honk at whoever is first in line. With fatigue permeating every bone and muscle beneath her skin, Reba believes that if she were to walk back to the thrift store right this minute, she would still be able to buy a box of day-old doughnuts. Moreover, she knows that if she were to do that, she later would not have to see the children's faces become sad with not-understanding. *For them,* she thinks, *each day is a world apart; each day is infinite and new, full disconnected from the past or the future.*

But when Reba finally decides, draws a deep breath and retraces her steps, her eyes suddenly catch sight of the man who works in the factory thrift store. Beyond the glass door he has appeared, materialized, small and arrogant; he glares at Reba from inside the shop, as if daring her to enter. The face she beholds is shrunken, cold. She imagines he is thinking that she does not have enough money even to buy a loaf of bread. Her fists clench in anger against him who is waiting, standing immobile inside the air-conditioned store; he reminds her of a smug figurine on display beneath a glass dome. In the town it is said he despises the poor people who buy his bread.

Reba hesitates. But it is not because of the money, nor even because of the shrunken, mean-faced man. She stops and turns again from the glass cage, recoils from the sterile factory because she is thinking, *No, I will not buy the doughnuts. I ain't going to protect Merle and Tommy from the truth that they ate the ones I brought home on Friday night.* She crosses the clotted intersection, her eyes watering with exhaust fumes, thinking, *I ain't going to protect Merle and Tommy from the consequences of what they have done.*

Under heavy-branched trees she walks; the hot sky is all but hidden. Across breathless shadows Reba now speaks indistinct words, speaking as she does whenever she feels the weight of the world upon her. "It ain't His way," she says. "Children ought not to suffer like that. Every day Merle forgets something he has just heard. It makes folks get mad. And he does not know why. He does not know why they are mad, so he ends up bellowing." With each step her hip feels stiffer. "It ain't His way for the children to suffer," she says.

And she looks up at the deep green leaves that form a tenuous bridge across the quiet street. From above the fluttering arch a sparrow sings; notes repeat and repeat until Reba begins to believe that if only she were to hear the sequence one more time, she would be able to decipher its message. Then the song stops.

She waits, listening, mouth slightly open. But the silence is flawless, intact, complete.

When at last she reaches her own front yard, the evening paper has already been thrown. She is twenty minutes late getting home.

The house has not been painted in over ten years. Shutters are gone from one of the downstairs windows, giving the front of the structure an odd, startled look—like a face that is missing an eyebrow. Reba used to worry about the shutters and the broken porch steps, but that was long ago. Now it is all too much a part of her to separate into worry; the house is as familiar as the faraway bark of a neighborhood dog.

Taking up the newspaper, she thinks, *It will be all right; it will.* Then she opens the heavy oak door.

She moves down the hallway, walking under the brass chandeliers. From everywhere in the kitchen the voices come: loud, clashing, unworded. Entering, she says, "Everybody quit yelling. Quit right now." The voices cease. She watches each of the faces recognize her. All strangeness melts away, disappearing into the smoke-stained corners of the kitchen.

"We 'bout ready to eat, ain't we?" Robert says.

With a wooden spoon he continues stirring the vegetable soup.

In that instant Reba wants nothing so much as to rest: to rest with her feet propped on an ottoman, lingering over the evening newspaper, not worrying, not having to wonder why there are only four people, instead of six, waiting for her in the kitchen. She closes and opens her eyes. The four others watch, as if expecting a surprise.

"Where are Merle and Tommy?" she says.

No one can remember; the kitchen empties of sound.

Then the telephone rings. And Reba can feel the vibration of it resonating between her shoulder blades. "Let Dwayne answer," she says. "Everybody let Dwayne; it is his turn to answer."

Dwayne walks over to the wall and takes the receiver from its cradle. He smiles into the phone before ever saying a word. "Hello?" he says. Next he frowns a little. "Wilson Cleaners?" he says.

"Tell them wrong number," Reba says, "and hang up."

Reluctantly Dwayne says, "It is the wrong number," and he gives up the telephone.

Moving between stove and sink, Reba puts the last of the dinner together. Although the telephone call was nothing more than a stranger's mistake, it has left her with a thin, discordant feeling, which she cannot shake. She hands a bundle of flatware to Sam, who works at the round table, allocating spoons and forks and knives to each of seven place-mats. Suddenly, looking surprised, he turns and begins counting aloud. At the number five he stops. He says, "It is suppertime, and Merle and Tommy are still outside."

All four of the men stare at her with fearful, scattered eyes. She has told them repeatedly that this is the time of day when people who are driving cars cannot see very well; she has always said that everyone in the family must be home by suppertime.

"Where are they, Reba?" Robert asks. "Where are Merle and Tommy?"

"I do not know yet," she says.

The youngest, Edward, who is not quite eighteen, begins to cry when he hears the words.

"It will be all right," Reba says. "Merle and Tommy will be here soon."

And she begins again to tell the unceasing story of living and of all that is alive. Her words form a smooth surface over the uncalm of the evening. She tells again about snow and Christmas, and about the blinking lights they always put on the tree that comes from a distant forest; she names the months remaining until they can take their money downtown to the stores near the bakery, where they will buy gifts for under the tree.

They quiet. Edward takes a handkerchief from his pocket and blows his nose. "I'm hungry," he says.

"Well then," Reba says, "I think we should probably go ahead and eat our supper."

Everyone sits down, and they hold hands to bless the food. Now the two empty places have lost their power to panic the four men, who are more like children than adults, yet not quite like children either. Reba watches them eat crackers and bowls of soup, thinking, *It is true. There is something special about people like us.*

After the meal, each tells a little about the day, beginning with Reba; tonight she tells about Mr. Simmons, and Robert smiles when his own name is spoken. Sam wants the next turn because this was his first day on the cleanup crew at the city park. Soon, at the table, there is bright, raucous laughter.

But as the kitchen clock moves inexorably through dusk into total darkness, Reba grows quite uneasy, quite scared.

The children are talking loud and at the same time.

She does not interrupt, however, because she does not want it to be Merle or Tommy's turn. Motionless, head bent and hands in her lap, she is thinking, *Now what? What now?* Reba knows that when anyone is missing without explanation, just missing, the children start remembering the hospital—what it was like for all those years—and then fear erases everything they have known of love.

The clock's second-hand consumes another minute.

She knows, too, that before long she will have to make a decision about calling the police or the emergency rooms. All around her the voices grow louder and louder; Edward looks hard at Reba. His thin face begins to form into a wordless bawl. "Hush," she says. And she says again, "Hush."

Then, as she is about to speak further, something happens. Amid all the table clamor, she believes she can distinguish another sound, this one from the front of the house: It is the sound of a door closing. "Oh God, oh God," she says softly, and she calls out, "Tommy? Merle?" Tommy answers; his voice travels down the hall, loping ahead of him. Next he is standing in the doorway. The red shirt sticks to his chest as if it were pasted on.

Reba looks at him. "Where is Merle?" she says.

"Here I am," Merle says, squeezing past Tommy. Both of them are out of breath.

Tommy says, "We fixed it, Reba. We done it all by ourselves." With his eyes he is smiling, watching her.

For a time Reba stares at each of them. Beneath the skin, her blood is pumping fast with the knowledge that they are safe, not hurt or in trouble.

In Merle's hand is a paper grocery sack. His eyes are wide open, solemn, undoubting, as though he has discovered a new and astonishing truth.

Everywhere it is quiet; no one speaks. The peculiar silence buzzes in Reba's ears. She cannot recall another time when the house has been so quiet, and it occurs to her that something is about to go wrong. It occurs to her that the room is now filled with the kind of silence that always precedes trouble. Merle and Tommy have not moved; they resemble children waiting for the start of some sort of game. Reba knows it is up to her: She must begin.

"Are you both all right?" she says.

"Yes," Tommy says. "And we fixed it." Merle does not say anything.

"Where have you been?" she says. "It's dark outside. What happened?" Then she stands up. Merle, with his face still expectant, pleased, hands her the paper sack, which is folded over at the top. He moves around the table to his place and sits down.

Standing in the room, holding the paper sack in her hands, she stands now as she once stood when the social workers came asking endless questions, making decisions about her. She opens the sack. Inside are two boxes of prepackaged doughnuts from the thrift store.

"For Sunday," Tommy says.

Yet his words do not synchronize with what already she knows to be true. "How did you get these?" she asks, knowing that neither Merle nor Tommy ever carries more money than a few coins for the telephone; they are paid by the sheltered workshop at the end of each week with a check, which they bring immediately home for her to deposit.

And her memory recalls the cold, shrunken man behind the glass door of the thrift store, the man who (it is said in the town) yells at poor folks and even chases them away when they don't have enough money to pay for the day-old loaves of bread. "Tommy," she says, "how did you get all these doughnuts?"

Unspeaking, Tommy seems to be rummaging his mind for something he has misplaced. He touches the front of his red shirt as if to determine whether or not it is still damp with sweat. Merle is clattering dishes at the table while he ladles soup into a clean bowl. He lifts his water glass and gulps it empty. The noise of his eating seems loud in the silent room.

Outside the screened window, moths have begun to collect; the evening sky has long since squeezed out the sun, and darkness now envelops the house like dense fog. There is clumped in Reba's stomach a sad, blurred fear. She thinks, *If they have stolen the doughnuts, if they have, I swear I don't know what I will do*. Her fear thickens when she recalls the trouble that resulted after Tommy took some comic books from the dime store one time without paying. And she is thinking, *The hospital will see this as the last straw. They will take Merle and Tommy away*. Then thoughts begin to clash, to hurtle against one another, seeking escape from the close heat of the room.

Putting the bag of factory-made doughnuts on the dinner table, she says finally, "Tommy, I have got to know exactly what happened. There is no running away from the truth. How did you and Merle get these?"

"The man just give 'em to us."

"Just gave you the doughnuts? Why?"

"I don't know why; but he did. Me and Merle fixed the mistake. The man give us two boxes of 'em."

"Are you sure?" she says.

"Yes," he says. "Two whole boxes."

"What I mean is, are you sure he gave them? I have never known that man to give away anything."

Like a match striking, flaring against a rock, there comes over Tommy's features a sudden look of bewilderment and rage. "We did not steal!" he shouts, his voice angry and hurt. "He give 'em to us!"

Merle stops eating; his eyes grow dark, cloudy.

"Merle," Reba says, but she is too late. It begins with one long sound like a murmuring sigh, which increases and increases until, at last, it becomes a loud, abject, wailing cry. What she hears is an uncanny moaning sound that will not quit, a voice, inarticulate, that encompasses the entire scope of human emotion.

Around the table Reba moves, hushing the others, moving to where Merle sits bellowing. She places the palm of her hand, cool and light, upon his forehead. As she touches the hot, damp skin, she recalls how, when Merle first came to live with them, he spent most of the time sitting on the floor

45

in a corner of his room; he would sit, hugging a pillow, watching her out of dull, uncomprehending eyes. And she would talk to him for hours at a time, knowing that inside of Merle was a delicate, tentative mystery she could never reach, knowing that only once in a while did he ever comprehend the total and undisturbed love she offered.

Now, remembering, waiting, with her palm still held on Merle's forehead, she hears Tommy's voice. "There is a note," he says loud, over the moaning. "Merle, where did you put the note?"

Merle quits bellowing. His face goes motionless, flat. "I don't know," he says and pulls away from Reba, sliding his chair across the floor with a harsh, thick, grating noise.

"Look for it," Tommy says. "Look in your pockets." To Reba he says, "We did not steal. The man give us the doughnuts and said to bring you a note." He looks then as though he wants to run away. "Reba, if the note is lost, . . . are me and Merle in trouble?"

She rubs her temples with the tips of her fingers; the hip joint aches worse than ever, and the kitchen still feels as if it will explode. "It is not God's way for little ones to suffer like this," she says. But she does not answer Tommy's question.

She tells Sam and Robert and Dwayne to wash the supper dishes. She takes a chair out from the table and sits close to Merle. "Merle," she says quietly, "look in all your pockets. Everything is all right. Just be sure to look in all your pockets."

After a time two quarters and a piece of string are laid on the oak table, along with a key ring. Then, at last, from the back pocket of his blue jeans, Merle takes a crumpled piece of paper. Opening the paper, smoothing it on the table, he says, "There is writing on it. What's it say?"

Without looking further, Reba knows. It is a bill for the doughnuts, made out in a cramped hand by the man at the thrift store. "Why, it's a bill," she says.

Tommy peers at the paper, his eyes puzzled, almost sullen. "The man give 'em to us," he says, and Merle repeats it: "He give 'em."

"No," Reba says, her heart suddenly unburdened. "He sold them to you. He trusted you to take the doughnuts without paying—trusted you to bring me a bill. It is a different kind of gift, better than if he had let you have them for nothing. Don't you see?"

"Are we in trouble?" Tommy asks. It is as if he has not heard the words.

She sighs and stands up. "Definitely not," she says. "There is no trouble. You and Merle got us some doughnuts for Sunday." She looks hard at Merle, then at Tommy. "Are you two going to be OK?"

But it is neither Tommy nor Merle who answers; it is Edward, the youngest, who continues sitting at the dinner table, now rocking back and forth. Edward utters a long series of syllables that do not make sense.

"What? What's wrong?" Reba asks while the sad, inarticulate rocking grows more and more urgent.

Next and immediately she remembers. Because of her fear about Merle and Tommy, it has entirely escaped her: In the evenings, when darkness begins to embrace the house, they always pause while Edward goes down the long hall and turns on the yellow porch light. For him, who has little control over his hands and cannot wash dishes or serve food or even make up beds, the entire day culminates in that moment. He has learned to turn on the porch light, and every day he waits, eager and hopeful, for Reba to tell him to do it. And each time it is as if she were telling it for the first time. But tonight the world went topsy-turvy, out of balance. So now he sits rocking and muttering in complaint.

"Edward," she says, as everyone stops to listen, "the porch light means welcome to all strangers. In the Bible it says: 'I was a stranger and you welcomed me; therefore, let your light shine always, into all the world.' "

Edward nods; he ceases rocking.

"Will you please turn on the porch light?" Reba says. "It is a welcoming thing to do."

Smiling, Edward gets up from his chair and begins to walk down the hall. His movements are slow, ungainly, but soon he reaches the switch near the front door and clicks it on. The leaded glass window in the door warms with color. "Into all the world," Edward shouts. The words are formed as slowly and carefully as a child shapes a sand castle on the beach.

When the sound penetrates the hot, moist air of the kitchen, dispersing the weariness that Reba has not until now been able to overcome, she calls back to Edward, "Into all the world." Then the others, even Merle, say it too, over and over, until everyone begins to laugh.

Reba cannot sleep. The air in her room seems dead, suffocating, and she can hear water dripping somewhere. Finally she gets up, puts on the bathrobe that the children gave her two Christmases ago, and roams the house until she finds the leaky faucet. She listens at each of the bedroom doors, listening for the gathering and releasing of breath. Next she goes into the kitchen and turns on a light.

Upon the large, round oak table sits the brown paper bag Merle and Tommy brought home. "Doughnuts," she says, and sinks down into one of the straight-backed chairs, thinking, *How can I carry it? Whatever will happen to them?* Moths flutter and thump against the window, while inside the kitchen a fly buzzes.

For a time, while the earth scuttles across deep space, and Reba worries or dreams or prays, there is a sense of too much reality, not too little. And she sits quite still, motionless, without knowing whether or not she is dreaming, staring at the bag of doughnuts. She can hear Merle's feet and then Tommy's feet, and they come on down the hall to the kitchen door and Merle stands there with the tears flowing quietly and his mouth wide, getting ready to bellow. At once she begins to fight herself out of sleep, saying, "Merle, don't yell," just in case it is not a dream. And it seems to her that it is immediately (yet she is aware of time passing) that Tommy, covering his ears with the palms of his hands, pushes past Merle into the kitchen. "Don't yell, Merle," she says again, loud, "Please don't," and to Tommy she says, "What happened? Why is he scared?"

"Oh," Tommy says. "Oh, oh, oh." His ears are covered and his eyes now are shut; he is jumping up and down.

Then Merle's outcry reaches across the night.

"No," Reba says. "No. It was only a bad dream. Everything is all right; you are home and safe. Tommy, for heaven's sake, what happened?" She is moving without even knowing she has left the chair, saying to the others who have begun clustering in the hall, Sam and Robert and Dwayne and Edward, "It is Merle having a bad dream." And she searches

50

each of their faces, asking, "Does anyone know what happened?" But no one speaks.

"Tommy, for heaven's sake!"

"What?" he says. His voice is trembling, not innocent.

"Tell me," she says, "right now."

"Well, . . . maybe I said we were in trouble for the doughnuts," he says. "Maybe I talked about the hospital a little."

Now, with the bellowing still loud and wild and fierce, and the others gathered around, Reba honestly believes she herself is going to cry. "Good Lord, I don't know what to do or think," she says and she sits back down; her body feels as if it has been drained of blood.

Slowly Merle grows quiet. He looks at Reba.

She turns toward him, sort of shaking her head, saying, "Please sit down, Merle. No one is in trouble. No one."

Confused, mournful, Merle sits down. He says, "But the man did not give 'em to us." On his face she can see the struggle to understand, the painful attempt to fathom something that is just barely out of sight. Then Reba takes hold of his hands, and her heart feels heavy, scared for the children, the ones who live as though they are being carried along by a savage and mysterious flood, unattached to the earth by either memory or time, buffeted and affronted and uplifted: all without apparent reason.

She says, "He did not give them to you. But he trusted you to pay for them later. No one is in trouble; not you, not Tommy."

"I forgot," Merle says.

"Yes," Reba says, "you forgot, that's all."

And immediately it is gone. As abruptly as it arrived, the shadowy fear dissolves from Merle's face. Reba can sense the tension leave him. "Is it Sunday?" he asks.

Robert says, "It is too dark outside to be Sunday," while the others murmur and whisper and look around at the bright electric lights in the room.

"I want it to be Sunday," Merle says. He is dejected, lost, downlooking.

Because she can hear the early sounds of summer birds, and because they are all safe for now, Reba stands up, walks to the window, and opens wide the kitchen curtains. "Well now," she says, "would you look at that."

And then they all stand there, watching the pale, nascent sun on the gray horizon; it is as though they are witnessing creation, the emergence of something out of nothing, the nativity of an absolute miracle.

With her eyes on the horizon, beholding the steady and faithful dawn, Reba says quietly, "If Merle will make the coffee, we can have hot cups of coffee with our doughnuts."

"It's Sunday," Merle says. "Ain't it, Reba?"

"Yes," Reba says, still watching the dawn, smiling, even laughing a little; "It is Sunday," she says. *It is Sunday*, she thinks, wiping her eyes with the back of her hand. *It is Sunday and we are going to have our doughnuts.*

LITANY
OF HOPE

God the Creator,
Have mercy on us.
God the Redeemer,
Have mercy on us.
God the Sustainer,
Have mercy on us.
Holy Trinity, one God,
Have mercy on us.

O Giver of all that is, hear the voice of your broken people. Hear us when we cry out to you in our finitude and pain; have pity on your creation.

For homeless children who live amidst broken glass and squalor and fear, growing daily more desperate and suicidal, we pray to you.
Hear us, O God of Life.

For lost generations of urban poor, women and men cut off from their dreams and caught in a net of explosive violence, we pray to you.
Hear us, O God of Life.

For families whose separation from their farms, and from the good earth they have nurtured and loved, is punctuated by the harsh sound of an auction gavel, we pray to you.
Hear us, O God of Life.

For children born to drug-addicted mothers, children who will come into life afraid of being human, we pray to you.
Hear us, O God of Life.

For the marginal, the desperate ones, who are crushed by a fluctuating global economy; for those who struggle daily to survive; for the people who have discovered that their trade or education or skill has become obsolete, we pray to you.
Hear us, O God of Life.

For whole species of animals that are repeatedly sacrificed to the god of profit-and-loss until at last they are erased from the face of creation, we pray to you.
Hear us, O God of Life.

God of our forebears, you are refuge and judge, shatterer and comforter. Open our hearts that we may discover your presence in all creation. Deliver us from the damnation of complacency and spiritual death.

LITANY OF HOPE

For the developmentally disabled ones, who love without compromise or limit and for whom the world is new each day.
We give thanks to you and praise your name.

For children, whose lively presence so often expresses a word of grace to those whose lives have been damaged and scarred.
We give thanks to you and praise your name.

For the persistence and courage of men and women who battle within themselves the demons of mental illness.
We give thanks to you and praise your name.

For the discards of society—the poor, the alcoholics, the refugees, the prisoners—who remind us that we are not in control of our own destiny.
We give thanks to you and praise your name.

For those who refuse to give up on deteriorating neighborhoods so long as life still breathes in the midst of rubble and fire-gutted buildings.
We give thanks to you and praise your name.

For people of faith who choose solidarity with the suffering, the outcasts, and the homeless of the world.
We give thanks to you and praise your name.

For the vision and the voice of all prophets.
We give thanks to you and praise your name.

O sing with joy to the Holy One, who is alive in the shadows and at work in the darkness.
Blessed be God for evermore.

O sing with joy to the one God, who keeps watch over those in shelters and alleyways; who makes a solitary star to shine upon the birth of a Savior and the death of a gambler.
Blessed be God for evermore.

Shout with joy, lift your voice and sing. The Holy One, who is animallike, passionate, and personal, goes forth in an eternal carnival of light and of grace and of love.
Blessed be God for evermore.

Shout with joy, lift your voice and sing. The redemption of God flows as a stream of living water, creating symphony from the chaotic voices of earthly existence.
Blessed be God for evermore.

Rejoicing in the company of all the living who have ever lived, let us commend ourselves, and one another, and all our lives to Christ our God.
To you, Redeemer God.

LITANY OF HOPE

God, have mercy.
Christ, have mercy.
God, have mercy.

Let us pray.

Almighty God, hear our words of anguish and thanksgiving. We earnestly pray that you will bring us out of pain into joy, out of anger into understanding, out of fear into confident hope. Shatter our illusions of security with the holy insecurity of your Word. Teach us again that Christmas, the revelation of your steadfast love for humankind, is celebrated wherever grace triumphs over the world's separation. Give us faith that we might each day discover the promise of Christmas as we care for those who are rejected or forgotten or dispossessed.

May God's blessing of life and grace and wholeness be granted to us, this day and forevermore. Amen.

DECATUR

From the dust-colored town he walks; heat mires his body like thick, dark mud.

Beside the road, shading it, stands a row of ancient walnut trees, their broad and placid leaves motionless upon the weary afternoon. He does not look back. He goes on, unwavering, resolute, brushing repeatedly at his dark trousers with his hands. The road runs straight and soundless ahead, softened by the heat, stretching away through the trees and thick underbrush to a place where it angles and disappears. Behind him, as though behind some strange finality of summer, the implacable world waits.

He goes on, thinking, It will be soon now. I reckon it will be soon enough.

When he comes to the place where the road turns, three barefoot children run past, careless and loud and wild. From the group a voice shouts: "Haaa-yooo!" He does not look at them. Within him a cough begins and dies and begins again; his breathing makes shrunken, rasping sounds. A short distance away, where the road curves, the earth appears to slant suddenly downward, away from the thin, silent ribbon of pavement. Traces of noise, dissonant and mechanical, drift up from some unseen source, mixing with the hot, still, breathless air.

Decatur Smith crosses the road; his bones feel quite brittle now, as though they will snap if he moves too quickly. An eroded wooden staircase, gray with age, leads from the hillcrest to a broad field below. When he reaches the staircase, he stops, listening to the babel of hammering and clanging. Far below he sees the dense July heat giving birth to an extravagant act of creation; the field burgeons with peculiar contrivances: giant spiderlike machines, wheels within wheels. With terrific bursts of color, tents and banners and painted signs are coming to life.

And yet, for all of that, the carnival has a sad, unfinished look about it.

From the pocket of his white shirt Decatur takes a package of cigarettes; he removes one. Carefully replacing the package, he begins twisting and pinching the cigarette in his hands, squinting against the sun. His suit is black, of almost formal cut; he wears a tie and a wide-brim Stetson hat. There is a vaguely ruthless quality about him, in the mouth and in the eyes. He twists and pinches the cigarette, watching the carnival grounds. Then from his coat pocket he takes a wooden match, which he snaps with a thumbnail until the match bursts into flame. He lights the cigarette and smokes without once taking it from his mouth. He does not move. It is as though he intends to wait there forever, or at least until the rides assemble themselves and the midway blazes into a chaos of noise and motion.

Behind him comes the sound of an automobile traveling along the road. He steps onto the downward-sloping stairway without hesitation; it seems to him almost as if his whole life has been leading toward this simple, dreamlike moment. His hand grasps the rough wooden banister. As he descends, he imagines that long ago someone must have fashioned the now-worn stairs with extraordinary care, sheltering the supporting framework deep within the cut-out hillside.

Standing on the field, feeling the white shirt tight with sweat across his back, Decatur stands as he did on the hill above: silent, remote. With a certain narrowness he seems to be watching the air, the afternoon, like a person who is waiting for some perplexing dilemma to be resolved.

Then he throws the cigarette down and begins walking toward the carnival midway.

Had he entered the field by the main gate he would have seen the sign: A Carnival For All Ages. But Decatur did not see the sign, or the gate either. And now he is not even thinking about the carnival; he is wondering what day it is. He decides it is Friday, thinking, Yes. Friday. I reckon that would be right. And he goes on, crossing the field, following the rutted path, thinking, It will be soon now, very soon.

Upon reaching the midway, he stops.

WOLF

What he sees before him is a man of uncertain age, with pale eyes that are almost transparent. There is something odd, something shadowy, about the man. Arms folded on his chest, he resembles an exotic figure that might have been carved on the facade of an ancient temple of the East. Even his blue work shirt and faded denims do not seem fully real.

Decatur watches the man's eyes. "Look here," he says, "I don't want trouble. No way do I need trouble."

Standing motionless, the other appears to be looking through and past Decatur, his pale eyes unwinking. "What's that you've got in your hip pocket?" he says.

Decatur keeps both hands at his sides. "It ain't a gun," he says, "if that's what you're thinking."

"Don't tell me what it isn't," the man says. "I don't want to know what it isn't."

"It's whiskey," Decatur says.

The man says nothing.

All around, the carnival has fallen quiet; the diesel engines have quit; it is a time out of time. Decatur feels as if something from another realm is bearing down on him, pressing in on him, like the thick July heat, thinking: This is not really happening. I am back at the rooming house having liquor dreams, that's what. He fumbles at his tie, watching the spectral figure of the other. When he finally speaks again, his voice is uneven, rough. "I don't drink on the job," he says.

"Job? What job?" the man says.

An ancient calliope wheezes abruptly, suffocating the sound of their voices.

Decatur shouts. A thread of sweat travels down the side of his face; he wonders if the shouting will make any impression at all on the shrill air. "—so I can maybe get out of this rotten town!" he is yelling when the calliope finally stops.

Without moving from the rutted path, the man turns his head. "Drunks get fired, not hired," he says.

"I'm not a drunk," Decatur says almost in a whisper. The pint bottle of cheap whiskey feels hard against his hip and he senses the carnival moving once more with sluggish progress as if readying for an early evening show call. Within him the blood races, and he is thinking, Durned if I can see why I don't just quit talking right now, saying aloud: "Look, I've worked plenty of joints before. I can gaff 'em or run 'em straight, makes no never mind to me. The thing is, I've got to get me a stake. C'mon, mister. All I'm asking is a day's pay for a day's work."

From beyond the midway comes a prolonged hissing sound. Attached to metal arms, miniature airplanes are slowly rising above the concession stands, rising and falling and then speeding up. For the first time Decatur removes his eyes from the unearthly face of the man; he watches the thrill ride as the dying sun glints off the wings of those sad, empty airplanes. Then a hot, greasy smell touches his nostrils, and he remembers he has had no food today. Yet hunger seems to be quite distant from him now, as if somehow it has taken on a separate existence, a hovering, invisible life of its own.

"Let's go, then," the man's voice says. "We're running out of time."

Decatur looks back toward the path. Where the other had been is nothing; he is gone. It is as if the man has been erased from the landscape. But the voice continues to resonate in Decatur's mind and the pale, undeviating eyes still seem to remain on him, who gazes up the midway then down, before ever seeing the man again.

Partially hidden by a group of early stragglers, the other waits, leaning a shoulder against the wooden frame of a concession, hands hanging loose at his sides. Then, apparently responding to an internal signal, the man turns and walks away. Decatur follows.

Without looking back or to either side, the man walks fast and with purpose through the carnival.

Decatur's black coat feels heavy on his back; sweat drops from his chin. Around the merry-go-round he hurries now, barely glancing at the painted animals. No music accompanies the peculiar clockwise gliding of horses and tigers and unicorns; their silent course seems eerie and wrong. Several young men linger near the closed ticket stand; one of them trips Decatur, who stumbles forward, arms outstretched; but his legs regain the ground and he goes on.

Ahead of him the man walks past the bottle pitch and the rifle range and the duck pond, after which his lean body vanishes between two concession stands.

Gripped by a strange urgency, Decatur starts to run. He runs between the two stands and finds himself suddenly behind the midway; it is as though he has crossed a kind of border. Slowing, he sees a row of trailers with clotheslines strung between them, and wash hanging on the lines. A sleepy, unhurried atmosphere has replaced the frenetic confusion of the carnival midway.

When Decatur at last catches sight of the other, it is to see him look back over his shoulder before entering a green-and-white-striped trailer. A small staircase made of wrought iron leads to the trailer door, above which is a lettered sign that reads: Carnival Office.

There is no sound except the fixed hum of an air conditioner, which rests in one of the windows of the office trailer; from it water drips onto the hardened earth.

Decatur moves with weary steps toward the door through which the man has disappeared. As he approaches, he notices that the broad green-and-white horizontal stripes have only recently been painted on the aluminum walls. He can almost smell the odor of fresh paint. Without conscious decision he allows his feet to carry him up the wrought iron steps until at last he stands directly in front of the striped door.

Perhaps because he has just finished running, or perhaps because his lungs are far from clear, Decatur's breathing is labored and his heart feels frenzied, large. He knocks on the door. The hollow knocking sound seems to be muffled by the unyielding heat.

From inside the trailer, a voice says, "It's unlocked."

Thinking, Well, here goes nothing; while he is also thinking, I sure could use a drink of whiskey, Decatur opens the door and goes in.

The room is not like any other he has ever seen; it breathes with a fragrance that is reminiscent of beginnings. Decatur takes off the wide-brim Stetson hat, and coolness touches his damp forehead. He draws in air as if he has too long been robbed of its nourishment. Then, squinting, his eyes encounter an amorphous, unshadowed dimness. "Ah," a distinctly female voice says, "you must be Decatur Smith, the notorious gambler. Do come in, Mr. Smith; do come right in."

For a full moment he cannot discern the origin of the transcendent, pneumatic voice; then a figure seems to form out of the cool fragrance. She is seated

behind a polished wooden desk; her garments flow
in vivid streams of color—stripes and patterns and
shapes, all mixing together into a wild, random, fantastic array. The beads around her neck give off a
darkish glow in the partial light, and her slender
hands move quietly about a small, open box that is
resting on top of the desk. Decatur cannot see what
the box holds, nor can he yet read the woman's features. He believes, however, that he must somehow
have met her before, must have held conversation
with her under some prior circumstances wherein
he told her his name; thinking: But where, I wonder?
Where was it?

"Won't you please sit down, Mr. Smith?" she
says, beckoning him to a chair.

It's a dream; I know it is, he thinks as he sits down,
placing the Stetson on the carpeted floor next to the
chair. A profound weariness engulfs his feet and legs
like the waves of an incoming tide. He is aware that
she continues to speak, but his ears no longer can
order the sounds into syllables, into meaningful
words. It is as if he has listened already to a lifetime
of words and simply can listen no more. Around
him the woman's voice floats, ephemeral as a blos-
som and eternal as the sky.

His eyes follow the tranquil movement of her
hands; gradually he perceives that she is arranging
cotton wool in the box on top of the desk, arranging
cotton around the motionless body of a small bird,
a sparrow. And it seems to him that he can almost

see the creature breathing, even though the bird's eyes are closed and its throat is silent.

He finds himself answering a question he does not recall having heard. "Las Vegas," he says. "I'm headed for Las Vegas, soon as I can get up enough money for bus fare."

The woman moves her head slightly, and Decatur sees a gleam of gold, perhaps from a comb, among the dark strands of her hair. Then it seems that the gold itself has become a source of energy, emitting an eerie, transient shower of light. Micalike fragments sparkle and scatter throughout the room. "Las Vegas?" she says. Her eyes are half-closed, and she appears to be contemplating something infinitely sad or regretful. She raises one arm, thereby causing a multiplicity of bracelets to chime like miniature Asian bells. Her manner bespeaks a wild stateliness, a sense of knowing secrets that blood and bone cannot discern.

"Eddie," she says, "don't you and Mr. Smith have some business to discuss?"

A sudden flicker of motion occurs to Decatur's left, and there appears the man from the midway, the ghostly one with pale, transparent eyes. He stands quite close, closer than before. "Look, Smith," the man says. "I'm China Eddie Dunn, the patch of this outfit. And I take care of whatever needs taken care of. You wanted to talk about a job, right? So let's talk." He seems less shadowlike than he did outside on the midway, as though he were gradually taking on substance.

"What can I tell you?" Decatur says. "My old man was a carney. And I know the ropes. I've worked joints and grab-stands and every kind of ride there is."

China Eddie Dunn says: "Yeah? Well, that's OK by me. Only this here is no gilly outfit that burns the lot and then disappears. You'd best be clear about that up front." The pale eyes and thin face do not betray an age; the man seems to live apart from the decay of time.

"I can run it straight," Decatur says.

"Sure; but do you?"

"I know how. And I will, if that's the call." Then, without knowing exactly why, he adds, "I'm headed for Las Vegas soon as I get a stake together." His voice lowers to a hoarse whisper. "What I need is a little traveling money, that's all." He looks across the dim, fragrant room and toward the polished desk. Perhaps he expects the woman to say something, or to resolve his growing sense of unreality with a movement of her eternal hand. But she does not look toward him; her entire attention is consumed by the small, breathing creature in the wooden box. She holds a medicine dropper to the tiny beak, which opens at the first touch of liquid. The sparrow gulps once, twice. Then with a terrific upsurge, its throat sounds a small, shrill cry; the once motionless body rights itself, and a crescendo of

71

sound like the flapping of enormous wings invades the room.

Simultaneously another shower of gold-flecked light scatters around Decatur, who, at that moment, believes he could actually touch the outer limits of everything he knows and everything he does not know. And he desperately wants to tell of it, to explain it to someone before he forgets—but he feels utterly incapable of movement or speech. Meanwhile, with infinitesimal shards of light still scattering, with the sound of flapping wings growing louder and louder in his ears, the room suddenly removes itself, melts, disappears from around him.

In the next instant he is standing outside on the midway and it is night.

Decatur blinks several times. Because it seems to him that the blinking will serve to clear his eyes, and he will once again be seated in the green-and-white trailer. Or maybe he will find himself back in the rooming house awakening from an all-night drunk. Maybe that's it, he thinks, an all-night drunk. But nothing alters; he remains on the midway: solitary, uncomprehending, in the midst of what appears to be endless light and noise. Carneys call out to the ever-moving crowd, and children laugh and scream as they are carried higher and higher into the air by the thrill rides. Decatur thinks: It is a dream; it must be. There is no earthly explanation otherwise. But what a strange dream. I must have really tied one on last night to bring all this about.

"Hey, mister!"

Decatur looks toward the voice. A shabby little girl is staring at him. She wears a faded cotton dress, and her hair is long and unwashed and limp; it is held back on one side by a plastic barrette. "Hey, mister!" she says.

"You talking to me?" he says.

"Yeah," she says. "How about it? Have you seen a monkey anywhere around here? I'm looking for my monkey." In her eyes he sees reflected the dizzy rainbow of the midway: Red and blue and green lights follow each other as though captured in a kaleidoscope.

"A real monkey?" Decatur says. "Are you talking about a real monkey?"

"Oh, he is just a small one. But he will get sick if I don't find him."

"Get sick . . . ," Decatur says, taking a red bandana out of his pocket and wiping his face. "Well, I guess that's always the risk you run, isn't it?" He notices that the hem of the child's dress is uneven. "How in tarnation did you get hold of a monkey?" he says.

"He's mine," she says. "I didn't steal him. I didn't. I am not like those kids who hang around Depot Town." Her eyes are cornered, suspicious.

Decatur puts the bandana back and looks at his hands. Having gone all day without a drink, he expects to see the familiar unsteadiness, the trembling. But his aging, gnarled hands are quite steady, quite calm.

"Hey, mister," she says. "Why are you looking at your hands?"

He turns full attention back to the girl as though to make absolutely sure that she is not an apparition. And peering thus at the dusty child-figure, he senses something of an uncanny bond or connection between them; it is almost as if she were waiting for him—just him—to show up in this odd, dreamlike place. Above them the airplane ride ascends and dips, while the late-night crowd continues moving on down the midway, past the loud-calling hawkers.

Decatur says, "I wonder where that little monkey could have gone to?"

The girl rubs her nose. "I'll bet it's this way," she says, and merges into the swarm of passersby.

"Wait!" Decatur shouts. "Give an old guy a chance to catch up!" And soon he is walking beside her. "You never told me what's your name?" he says.

"Folks call me Eudalia," she says. (She pronounces it u-dale-ya.) "Who are you?"

A peculiar weightlessness comes over Decatur; his words seem to originate from a place outside of himself. "I'm a professional gambler, I guess," he says. "I mean, that's what I do. The name's Decatur Smith." Behind his eyelids, somewhere apart from the midway, he can even now see the felt-covered tables peopled with men and women who are smoking and playing dead-earnest cards, playing for high-stakes money, and with their revolvers hidden from sight: But now the play has come around to him and he must decide whether to raise or to fold or to call.

He thinks: This is like dreaming in the middle of a dream. I wonder if I will remember any of it when I finally wake up. In his back pocket the pint bottle of whiskey feels like a small, hard relic or an ivory god whose function has all but faded from memory.

"You're a card player, ain't you?" Eudalia says.

"That's right," he says. "Straight poker, five-card draw—and that's all. Taken me a whole lifetime to learn the game. But, yes, I'd say I'm a card player." He smiles a crooked smile and removes a cigarette from the package in his shirt pocket. "Now you tell me something, will you? That little monkey: How was it you managed to come by it in the first place?" He asks the question, but when he speaks, his head is back-tilted, staring far beyond the lights of the midway and the rides, gazing now at the wild, lambent stars. Out of habit, he searches for the Big Dipper and for all of the other constellations he learned to identify while yet a child, during those dusty times on the open road when he and his father would sweep the heavens to find such familiar shapes, during the lonely, powerless nights between towns. But tonight there is something odd going on; the stars are not arranged in anything like the usual ways—

they form entirely new designs against a strange black sky. The moon has not yet risen. And directly overhead, there shines a solitary star of terrific brightness. "I don't get it," Decatur says. "This is downright crazy."

"What's crazy, Decatur Smith?" Eudalia says. She is looking at the sky now, too.

"The stars," he says. "They ain't any of them where they ought to be."

"But I see lots of stars—all over the sky."

"Sure. It's just that they ain't in the places where they always are."

"Does it matter?"

"Well, you'd think . . . ," he says. And then he says, "Oh, I don't know; maybe it doesn't matter. Why would the sky make any more sense than the rest of it?"

Wondering if he will ever wake up from this strange, unmanageable dream, Decatur replaces the cigarette in its package, without having thought to light it.

"Now are we going to look for my monkey, Decatur Smith?" Eudalia says. "Are we?"

Suddenly the accumulated weariness of sixty-odd years whelms him like flood waters, and he says, "Hey, why me? Why me to help you look for some zoo-type animal that may or may not belong to you anyway? Huh?" The words rasp across the radiant night. He ceases talking, expecting her to turn away

from the fading, weary bitterness of his spent life.
Calliope music fills the gap where his voice was.

Indomitable, waiting, the girl denotes no surprise
whatsoever in her posture or facial expression. "It's
my monkey," she says.

She looks at him; they look at each other. Then
they walk together down the midway again, with
Eudalia in the lead. She moves easily through the
carnival, her bare feet faithful to the dusty path. It
is as if she is quite unfettered by anything earthly.
Decatur, following, can feel a peculiar change starting to take place within him. As he walks he can
feel it: The sad effort of living, the ineradicable
wrongs he has done, and the failures, the myriad
failures—all seem to be flowing from him, swirling
away, gradually dissolving under the tenuous multicolored strands of light from the midway. He is
certain now that he must have stepped outside of
ordinary existence. Nothing and everything looks
familiar to him. In fact, he is even thinking that he
has worked this carnival before. He is thinking that,
ever so long ago, he actually stood behind one of
these very same concessions, calling out to the customers, talking the talk.

The crowd has thinned. Decatur knows that soon
these people will return to town, to homes which
have broad, pleasant porches and yellow-lighted living rooms. He remembers the eight-dollar room he
has inhabited for the last few months—the most recent in a long series of cheap rented rooms. A cough

rises up in his throat, but it never takes shape. Instead, while gazing once more at the wild, infinite sky, he hears his own voice saying, "Las Vegas, Nevada. Now, that's where I belong."

Walking slower, Eudalia says: "Where's that? Where is Las Vegas? And how come you belong there?"

"Out west," Decatur says. "And I belong there because it's the only place I know that never gives up the daylight. In Las Vegas it's always the middle of the day—and anyone, absolutely anyone, can end up wearing a diamond stickpin won fair and square at the poker table."

"Diamonds!" Eudalia says. "Real ones?"

"Oh, yes," Decatur says. "Real diamonds."

A low whistle comes from the child. "You must be pretty lucky at cards, Decatur Smith. I used to play poker with my pa lots of times, but luck never did run my way."

"No, not luck," he says. "Don't go believing in luck." The words are easy and natural, like those spoken to a confidant in front of an open fire. "That's what happened to me the first time I was in Vegas. Maybe it was the desert air, or maybe it was being only thirty-six years old. I don't know. Anyway, I got to believing in luck. And what happened was this: One night I walked into my hotel room and took a punch right in the face from some guy who must've waited for me there all night. Blood came out of my nose, and I nearly blacked out. Sure,

DECATUR

I was carrying a gun—a Smith and Wesson .38—but by the time I grabbed for it, the guy had already taken my money and gone. I lost over ten thousand dollars cash." He pauses then, listening.

From the warm, lighted carnival comes the usual clashing of noises. The calliope wheezes and hawkers direct their ceaseless, rapid talk to the thinning clusters of people who stand idle in front of wooden concession booths. In that instant, through and beyond the familiar cacophony, Decatur hears a new texture, as if all the dissonance were gradually transforming itself into some evanescent and mysterious symphony.

Eudalia's bare feet move silently along the dirt path. Facing forward, she says, "I don't understand. Why would you want to go back to Las Vegas? Someone might punch you out again and take your money like before!"

"Ah, the game's in my blood, Eudalia," he says. "I don't reckon you can likely imagine how exhilarating it is to be sitting at a no-limit table with real class players. It took me fourteen—no, it was fifteen years of small-stakes games and working carney joints before I ever saw Las Vegas. Then, I lost my nerve after that guy bushwhacked me—and I drifted back east. Even tried to give up the game, give up poker. But it's no good. I've got to get back to Vegas. Got to get back at least one more time before they plant me." He draws a long breath of fresh air, thinking, *Soon now, it will be soon enough. At that* moment he believes he is on the verge of discovering something hidden and astonishing and profound, but whatever it is manages to elude him.

Then they are behind the calliope. A carney wearing a bright yellow shirt sits on a raised bench playing the giant keyboard; he scowls at them like an old, protective dog; he seems to have been partnered to that organlike machine for at least a hundred years.

Nearby stands the merry-go-round that Decatur passed earlier when he was running after China Eddie Dunn. While watching the brightly painted animals circle and bob to the music, he suddenly realizes what it was that had bothered him about this particular carousel. "Clockwise," he says.

Eudalia is not paying attention. She hums along with the calliope, once in a while hitting the correct notes. "What about clocks?" she says.

"No," he says, "clockwise. The carousel is going clockwise and I ain't never seen one do that. All the carousels I ever seen went counterclockwise."

But before he can listen to Eudalia's response, before even he can take another breath, the merry-go-round is utterly forgotten. His eyes are caught by, riveted upon, a sign in front of the concession stand immediately to the right of the carousel. "Eudalia," he says, "look!"

She looks. And she reads aloud the sign. "Duck Pond Game. Everyone a Winner. Decatur Smith,

Proprietor." She raises her voice to be heard over the music. "Hey, that's you, Decatur! That's you!"

A shiver travels from his scalp all the way down to his toes. "This here's a mighty weird dream," he says.

"Oh, you ain't dreaming," Eudalia says, moving around the carousel until she is standing directly in front of the concession. "It's a real booth, with a real duck pond! C'mon, let's start it up!" she says. Her face is full of child-anticipation. She stands on tiptoe as though to see better. And to those who pass by she beckons and calls out: "It's not too late to choose a prize! Everyone is a winner here—it's not too late! Stop and play the duck pond game!"

Curiously, with each gesture of the child's arm, Decatur thinks he can almost hear the faint melodic chiming of Asian bells, the same sound he heard in the trailer. But then, as he tries to listen more carefully, whatever it was he heard merely vanishes into the dust of the carnival.

Decatur takes his place behind the counter, and about two dozen people gather. He touches the rough, painted planks of wood that form the booth. Beneath his fingers, the painted wood seems to take on breathing life. And he is remembering all of the joints that he has ever worked, or that his father had ever worked. He thinks: This one contains all the others within it. Yes, all of the others are contained within this one. Across the back wall are shelves on which sit stuffed animals and penny whistles and combs and radios. In front of him is the duck pond itself—a narrow band of water that, at the moment, lies motionless, calm.

Eudalia says, "I'll show you how to work it," and she points to a toggle switch near one of the back shelves.

He flips the toggle switch. The water starts moving and splashing like a natural brook; it, too, seems alive. Now the steady current of water carries dozens of small carved ducks from one end of the counter to the other. Each duck has been decorated in a different way; no two are alike. "This sure ain't what I expected," he says, "when in town I seen them posters stapled to telephone poles and telling about a carnival at the fairgrounds. I just figured to get me some roustabout work. I never figured it would be anything like this."

From across the living stream of water Eudalia says, "Do you know how I knew where to find that toggle switch?"

Decatur shakes his head, and he searches under the counter, finding a canvas apron with pockets deep enough to hold an evening's worth of nickels and dimes and quarters. He puts the apron on; it fits exactly.

"I knew because I thought it out," she says. "I've got a good head on my shoulders and I think for myself. At home we have a glass display case and in it are five blue ribbons that I got for knowing how to think." Eudalia moves from side to side, swaying sort of, while behind her Decatur can see the timeless blinking of the carnival lights. Then she says, "Decatur Smith, can I have the first turn at the duck pond?"

The small, silent crowd of people draws closer, their faces expectant of some curious and signal event. Decatur hands Eudalia a net, with which she scoops from the water one of the decorated carved ducks. On the bottom of the duck is painted the number one.

"Why, that's absolutely the best number," he says. "It's your choice. You can choose any prize at all that's on the shelves."

"The monkey," she says, pointing.

The assembled crowd makes a sound like the rustling of trees or the movement of wings through thin, autumn air.

Decatur turns around. To his surprise, there sits on the topmost shelf a light brown monkey. Its small face is more human than animal, more eternal, perhaps, than human. The monkey's hair has an eerie, luminous quality, as if the creature were somehow fashioned out of light and dust and clouds. Gazing now into the animal's unwinking round eyes, Decatur stands utterly mesmerized, turned inside out. He sees at the center of the eyes a strong, clear flame, through which moves a series of incomplete, phantomlike shapes. And it occurs to him that he is watching all the events of his life pass through that curious flame—being first tempered, then forgiven, then restored.

Apparently without moving at all, the small monkey disappears from the shelf and reappears on Eudalia's shoulder. Eudalia looks pleased, knowing, unastonished. And when she strokes the iridescent hair of the animal, a rainbow trembles in the air around her.

"Well," Decatur says, "I reckon you found what you was looking for." Although to himself, he says, I will have to give up drinking whiskey completely if it's going to keep bringing on dreams like this one. And then it occurs to him that maybe he has moved beyond whiskey, beyond life itself even, but the thought is half-formed, incomplete.

Next and immediately he hears someone calling, "Eudalia, Eudalia," and sees a woman pushing to the front of the crowd. The woman continues crying out even after she is standing directly in front of the girl.

"I'm right here, Ma," Eudalia says. "No need to keep yelling for me. I'm right here."

The woman quiets. But her mouth remains half-open. The raw-boned body goes slack, hands limp at her sides. She is like a person who was born a little wrong, one who has never quite been able to catch up with her own living self. "I got lost," she says. "I didn't know where you was."

"I only went to find the monkey," Eudalia says. "How about it, Ma, do you want to play the duck

84

pond?" So saying, she appears older, almost regal, with the strange monkey settled on her shoulder. She tells Decatur: "This is my mom. I take care of her. We are waiting for Pa to get back. We been waiting a long time, and Ma gets kind of confused sometimes."

In Decatur's heart a dreamy sadness grows, and he looks away from the girl and her mother, looking upward at the single star that remains steady and uncompromising overhead. "It's a good thing you've got that head for thinking, Eudalia," he says. "It's a mighty good thing."

"How much?" the woman asks. "How much to play?" The bland expression has been replaced by vague worry.

"It's free," Decatur says and offers her the net.

But she does not take the net; she scoops one of the ducks out of the water by hand. Holding the decorated figure in cupped palms as if it were fully alive, she laughs, clear and loud, like a child on Christmas morning. For a moment it seems that the very music of the midway has paused, hushed, while she laughs; for the space of a heartbeat the calliope waits; then, once again, its sound swells around them.

Decatur does not ask to see the painted number on the bottom of the duck. Nor does he ask which prize the woman wants; he simply reaches to a shelf and selects a bouquet of fragrant white roses. These he hands to her as an additional gift, over and above the carved duck that she has already selected. He notices that the woman's teeth protrude from her mouth and her eyes are set wide apart in her broad face. Yet when she accepts the flowers, her smile is as beatific, as all-accepting, as a saint's.

The smile. The smile is the last thing Decatur remembers before he is encompassed, surrounded, by a massive scattering of light: myriad particles similar to those he experienced in the trailer. This time, however, the light is nearly blinding. And he is aware of rapid movement. He feels himself to be traveling within a pulsing stream of dazzling light. It is as if the disparate particles suddenly have come together into a wild, spectacular flow that is carrying him along, much as the stream of water carried the carved ducks. Now the carnival and the lights of the midway and the people are receding from him with incredible, extravagant speed. And he can no longer discern anyone, see anyone clearly enough to distinguish one face from another. He holds in his mind now only the memory of the mother's angelic smile.

From somewhere beyond the lambent suspension he most certainly can hear the delicate chiming of Asian bells, and he believes, he knows, that it is he himself who is being summoned. Then, with that harmonious sound still full in his ears, he sees again the woman from the trailer, the one who wears a garment of fantastic, multicolored fabric. The woman is holding a bouquet of white roses; on her shoulder sits the light brown monkey with its ancient, vivid, unearthly eyes. She is speaking to Decatur now, speaking in a voice that incorporates all the voices he has ever heard, male and female. "It's not too late to choose a prize, Decatur Smith," she says. "Everyone is a winner here. . . ."

With one hand she makes a waving motion that seems to indicate both farewell and welcome, while he continues traveling, receding, advancing, on the curious, pristine torrent of light.

When the sensation of movement quits, Decatur judges himself to be distant from the carnival, in a place he is well acquainted with. Under his feet he feels uneven pavement, and all around him, like something tangible, is the smell of decay.

As if looking through darkened glass, he studies his surroundings. The brick structures on either side he recognizes. Often he has stumbled through this ruined corridor when he was sick with losing and haunted by dark fear. He knows he has returned to the town, to the familiar alley between a secondhand clothing store and the old, crumbling pool hall that he frequents. He knows also that if he travels the length of the alley and turns right on Sixteenth Street, in half a block he will arrive at the rooming house where he rents a furnished room by the week.

For a while he remains there, standing quiet, listening to the vague and restless darkness. This is the part of town inhabited by the discarded, damaged ones. Here violence and risk are more visible than elsewhere. Here the reality of human self-destructiveness floats to the surface of knowing, of experiencing, as does a corpse in water.

He starts toward the rooming house. But he stops again, almost at the very moment he begins walking. Uneasiness grips him; every muscle tenses with dread. Whatever is out there, he can feel it through the darkness. And he knows he is not alone in the alley. But hard as Decatur stares, there is nothing at all for him to see, except the vacant brick walls and the crouching shadows.

Sweat begins to pour from him. He blinks several times, unable to determine whether he is sensing movement or some new and strange dream-effect. Then, as he watches, there is a curious shifting of light and dark, a pulsing of reflected images, a brief, fading gleam of silver. But Decatur's eyes are not quick enough to read the intricate language of shadow. It is only a primitive insight within him which discerns the presence of another in that suffering, lonely place.

For what seems like an eternity, he maintains mute vigil on the shadow and the light, standing motionless, as if he were a statue carved in an attitude of contemplation or of prayer. He watches until his eyes grow weary with the effort, though already he knows that whatever is waiting to reveal itself is not human, not a person. Down the desperate alleyway, amid the refuse of human life, he can feel it waiting, standing all untamed and powerful, while he continues to watch, and shapeless half-ideas blur the distinction between inner world and outer perception.

When at last he sees the wolf, it is not because it moves toward him, but rather because the shadows give way, parting suddenly like curtains on a stage. The great silver wolf stands unmoving, ancient, as though it has always been there, and Decatur just not able to see it. Nor does the animal appear to be ghostly; it partakes of solidity and of wholeness and of passion.

A breeze enlivens the alley. And something more than fear, something older and more profound than fear, flows like blood through Decatur's veins. It is almost as if he is watching the prying apart of the universe. The silver wolf makes no sound, but its presence bespeaks an irrevocable bond with creation, the intrusion of divine compassion into every dark and abandoned corner of existence.

From somewhere close behind him, he hears a man's voice. Startled, he glances over his shoulder and sees China Eddie Dunn, who is saying, "Hey, Smith, what's going on? What is it?"

His heart rapid, loud, Decatur looks immediately forward again. But all that remains is an interplay of light and shadow. The wolf has vanished, translated, into another place or dimension or realm. "You ain't going to believe it, Eddie," Decatur says, "but I just seen an enormous wolf."

WOLF

"A wolf?" the other says. "Is that what you said?"

"With my own two eyes I seen it," Decatur says. "Right here in this godforsaken alley. A wolf. I know for certain it was. And its fur was the color of pure silver. I ain't never seen anything like it." Then he realizes his whole body is trembling, and not from the effects of whiskey. For the first time ever, the shaking of his body feels as if something fantastic and new is being created within him.

China Eddie Dunn moves past Decatur. "C'mon, Smith," he says. "Let's step out." With even strides he travels down the alley toward Sixteenth Street.

Decatur's legs gain strength as he follows China Eddie. Then the two men are on Sixteenth Street. Then they are entering the rooming house, surrounded by the smell of cooked cabbage, and climbing fast the poorly lighted staircase to the fourth floor. No longer does Decatur have to stop at each landing with his lungs on fire and his heart feeling tight inside him; now he navigates the steps quite as easily as does his companion.

Outside the door to his room Decatur pauses. Searching his pockets, he says, "I don't seem to have my key. I must have left it on the dresser." In that instant an odd reluctance washes over him, and he wishes he were back at the carnival talking to Eudalia.

China Eddie Dunn says: "Try it. Try the door. Maybe it's unlocked."

The latch gives way when Decatur turns the handle. The door opens. But what he sees as he enters the room is not what he expects, not at all what he ever expected to see. At first he shrinks instinctively from the surprise of it, the shock of it even. Because what he sees by the light of the room's single lamp, lying on the sad, narrow bed, as quiet and as still as death, is himself.

On the bed he is lying nearly facedown, but the features are clear enough; they are his own features, except that they have been drained of life. He wears a black suit and tie and a white shirt with the collar loosened. On the floor nearby is an almost-empty whiskey bottle, which has fallen on its side. Without anyone telling him, Decatur knows immediately that the man on the bed must have died some several hours ago.

And although once he would have hated the life-less body, with upon it the scars of heavy drinking and of despair, now he does not. He feels completely at peace, as though what he sees there is no longer himself. In death, the body resembles the weary remnant of an existence that is neither wrong nor right, but which has already been born, received, into a new creation. Every regret and resentment, every pain and fear, has dissolved now like melting snow on a mountainside.

"He looks dead," China Eddie says.

Decatur straightens his shoulders, which no longer ache with age and dissipation. Now, standing upon the loosely planked floor of the room, he can see through the open and curtainless window the sky and the single, high, pale star that was over the midway. He can see, too, that it is almost dawn. "I'm ready," he says. And his heart is moved by an exhilaration greater than he ever felt in Las Vegas, or anywhere else on earth. "I'm ready now," he says.

Soon thereafter, through the open window, he hears the vivid, magic sound of a calliope. From the street below come the excited cries of children who are running and laughing, hurrying to see the traveling show as it enters the town. Without conscious thought Decatur knows that the carnival, carrying with it Eudalia and her mother and the duck pond and all the rest, has come precisely for him.

The music grows louder and more distinct.

Then, for the first and only time since Decatur has met him, China Eddie Dunn smiles. "They're expecting us, Smith," he says, turning. "C'mon, let's get this show on the road."

A SHORT POEM

God's
eternality entered
   the
   riskiness of
   earth.
The entire
created order was
   changed
irreversibly. And as
     the darkness was
   transformed, a
   single
        star
poured out divine
light.

It is frightening
     to be
   following a star,
not knowing where
   it is taking
   you,
or where it is
   shining, or

93

if you have
reached it yet.

Were stars then
so different from stars
    now? Could
        the Magi know
    with any certainty
where the
    starshine fell? Or
did they have
    to decide?
        How did
        they know it was
    not shining on
Bethsaida, or
        Joppa,
    or Nazareth?

HELEN

1

In the physical darkness the clattering wheels of the train roll on, pumping rhythmic along the tracks below. Then they pass the Somerset station. They have almost passed it. Looking, she can see the street lights of the town, all haphazard and delicate and beautiful across the earth. She can hear the echoing darkness as it rushes beyond even thought in the cold night air. Then they have passed Somerset. And she can remember how her father used to say that those who are human born are forsaken creatures of darkness from beginning to rotten end. She remembers, but she does not understand. And none ever to know how she did not as a child understand either, but made no denial when her mother cursed God and the Church and her dead father's Jesus faith. Though sometimes she thought she might tell her mother. She thought there would come a time when she no longer felt the outrage and hatred (if that be the word) and the rigid fear. In that quiet moment she would tell.

Now, with the shadow of winter upon her, she

is traveling to Thunder Bay, thinking, *It is the right thing to do*, and imagining herself talking quite calmly to a woman she has not seen for twenty-three years, saying, 'Mother, why won't you let me love you?' and all the while remembering, knowing, irrevocable sadness and shame. For an instant she fumbles with her eyeglasses, then folds them neatly into a soft case she has taken from her purse. Sort of looking ahead of herself, she seems to hover in an attitude of extravagant awareness.

The train is sullen with emptiness. She sits on a faded cloth seat that has been stained by the years into obscure, monotonous patterns. The air is stale. In the whole car there is only one other passenger. But she does not think about him. She is quiet, ignoring the sad, stale emptiness, the passenger, the overhead lights.

Something else there is she ignores. As unfading as remorse, it brushes at the edge of her consciousness. Yet she will not, cannot, acknowledge it.

Slowly she breathes in and out. The darkness and the overhead lights blur together into filmy gray. Now her thoughts are directed inward; they are homeward bound like the train. Tonight she will see her again: the mother of twenty-three years past, a woman wearing powder and rouge and a cotton print dress. For a moment it seems she can actually see her. But then the dream figure yields to the flat gray of not-seeing once more and is gone. Still she does not look at what is so close to her, part of her—

the marks, the red-brown lines on the inside of her left arm. Drawn carefully from wrist to elbow, the scars look like long rows left by a plow in fresh earth. If a person were to view it closely, the arm with its rows would reveal a terrible, methodical history. Some of the marks would be covered with crustings of clotted blood. Others would be flat and brown: striations from days, weeks, months ago, their symmetry revealing an awful and frightening precision.

But she is not aware of her arm. It is covered by the oxford cloth of the shirt. The arm rests lightly against her body, wrist down so that no one can see even that small portion of scarring not hidden by the sleeve.

Neither does the man look at her arm. From his jacket pocket, he takes a squashed package of cigarettes. Then he stirs in his seat. He smells of grease and sweat. "Excuse me," he says distinctly, though she does not look, refuses to look at him. He says, "Excuse me."

"What is it?" she says. "What do you want?" Her glance is quick and cold. She does not understand how he could possibly be part of the situation, the set of circumstances, to which she has been consigned.

Again he shifts in his seat, leaning in her direction. He says, "I was wondering . . . could I trouble you for a match? Or perhaps a lighter?" The cigarette is held between two stubby fingers; his hands are dirty.

"You shouldn't be smoking here," she says. "There's a sign; don't you see it?"

He says, "A lighter, perhaps? Or a match?"

She is not looking at him, but she can feel his eyes watching her. She believes he is staring at her now like he did when he got on the train at Chicago. First he walked, unsteady and alien, all the way through the passenger car. Then he stopped not five feet away and touched the brim of his slouch hat, and stared. Then he sat down heavily in the seat right across the aisle.

Too close, she thinks, *The whole train and he sits right across the aisle from me with his reek and his dirt and his cigarettes.*

"Excuse me," he says. "About that match . . . ?"

She reaches inside her purse. Her hand moves past the zippered compartments, past the eyeglasses case, to the very bottom of the bag. Under several old tissues she finds the lighter, touches its smooth metallic surface. She wonders how he knew she would have a lighter, thinking, *He couldn't have known. He didn't know.* Her hand closes around the smooth metal; she draws from her purse the lighter that was hidden from sight.

"I want it back," she says. She watches the man light the cigarette. Her eyes watch to see if his hands tremble, as she believes they must. But the hands are quite steady. She thinks, *The whole train and he sits right across the aisle, smoking, watching my every move.* Even so, she will not herself move to another seat. That would show she has feelings, cares about him, cares where he came from or where he is going.

"Thanks," he says and gives back the lighter.

Her hand takes it and drops it in her purse. The arm, with its rows of crusted wounds, still rests anonymously against her body. And all the while she is remembering everything as nearly as possible to the way it was twenty-three years ago and more, who is entering the dream-grayness that leads up a staircase to the apartment where the mother waits. Then suddenly it all rushes away. Her thoughts collide with the shrill voice of the train, and the woman starts.

Apparently the man does not notice. "You live around Thunder Bay?" he asks. Under the slouch hat he smokes without touching the cigarette, one eye half-closed against the smoke. The other eye is pale, canny, remote.

Beneath his voice she can hear the sound of running feet on uneven stairs. The back of her neck goes cold as she remembers the Christmas Eve when her father shouted and shouted at her mother, then knocked over the tree with its ornaments (while she, the child, stood amazed, uncomprehending), shouting at the mother because—wild, rolling—only because. *It was after that. It was after that*, she thinks, while saying aloud, "There's a sign. Don't signs mean anything to you?"

Perhaps he ascribes the hoarseness of her voice to the long, tiring ride; or perhaps he senses in it the dark and unyielding compulsion. "Why, yes," he says, "I believe in signs. Do you live in Thunder Bay?"

"Thunder Bay," she says. But the words carry no significance, symbolize nothing for her. She is thinking, *I am fifty years old*, remembering, *In a corner of the attic are piled white boxes and inside them the letters.* Worse than anything her husband hated the letters. Whenever he saw one, with its black pencilmark through the address and always the single word *Refused* penciled upon it too, he hated it. He told her, 'Leave well enough alone, Helen,' though he spoke to his newspaper, not to her, and she cannot leave well enough alone, because: *Every letter I ever sent her has been blackened, returned; so now I must travel to where she is, because that which was foreordained to be the design, the construct, of my life is not yet complete, and I am fifty years old.*

"I hate Thunder Bay," the man says, turning toward her. He puts one leg up on the seat. "No offense, lady, but if you live around there, you ought to move. Me, I'm in for a minute, then gone. Got a piece of business to take care of. That's the only reason I bother with the place." The words come in apparently endless succession. "Yes," he says, "Got a piece of business to take care of. Then I think I'll go down to Atlanta. Now there's a city. You ever been to Atlanta, lady?"

"Why are you talking to me?" she says. "What do you want? You're not even supposed to be here."

The man doesn't answer; an ash drops from his cigarette. He says, "Not supposed to be here?" and if change there is in his face, it is no more than a flicker. But both eyes are open now. "Not supposed to be here? Is that what you said?"

She is quiet, with her head turned a little, not caring what he says or thinks. The sound of his voice goes around her like dreaming, and although exactly this has never happened to her before, she is utterly calm, tranquil, alert. "I meant no harm," she says, thinking, *If only I were to look, he would be gone.* But something within her keeps her from looking.

"Say, are you all right?" the man says. "Are you?" His voice is not threatful or angry.

She says, "You ought not to speak. It would be better if you didn't."

"Why?" he says. "Because I'm not supposed to be here? Is that it?"

"Yes," she says. "And because this is not the way it goes. It would be better if you didn't speak."

"Well, can you beat that?" he says.

"Please," she says.

"I didn't say anything," he says. "How could I say anything? I ain't here. It ain't going like this; it's going the way you want."

"Please don't keep talking," she says.

"Can you beat that?" he says.

"You're only making it harder," she says. "What you say or do will change nothing. Nothing at all."

"OK," he says, "I understand."

She says, "I know you don't understand. But the hate in me must be reconciled. The hate must be expiated. It is the right thing."

The man flicks the cigarette into the shadows. He is unshaven and dirty, and his face looks strained, frustrated. "No, lady, it ain't the right thing," he says. "And whatever you're planning to do, it ain't going to happen the way you think. Believe me; I know."

She sits motionless, thinking, *He is pretending to be poor and uneducated, but he isn't. I wonder why he is pretending*. Then she takes on an attitude of irrevocable, righteous conviction. "After twenty-three years," she says, "I am on my way to see my mother."

The man's body moves like a gray mist, without speed or angularity. Suddenly he is standing in the aisle, his pale eyes looking like pieces of translucent crystal. "Take some advice from a real-life, time-serving drifter," he says. "Go on back home. Forget the whole thing. Just go back home before it's too late."

And she believes, *This is a man who flows into secret places and hurts people, a man who obliterates life*, thinking, *He collects his pay behind darkened, decayed buildings, then disappears*, while thinking, *The hate within me must be reconciled, expiated, atoned*.

"Ain't no good gonna come of it," he says, "you'll see." Then he says something she never could have expected, never would have believed, if she had not heard his actual voice uttering the quiet words. "Listen, do me a favor and pray about it," he says. "You can at least do that. Am I right?"

For a long moment she does not answer.

"Well?" he says. "Will you or won't you?"

"I . . . guess so," she says. "I mean, yes."

Then he is gone. The space where he stood has emptied itself of him. He is not lurching down the aisle, bumping into seats; he is not anywhere. She puts out her hand as if to clear away a haze, then closes her eyes. She is still sensing him, thinking about him, when behind her a door opens, letting into the car a roaring, rushing sound. By the time the cold air reaches her, the door has clanged shut. She tries to block out all memory of the man, but though she is not yet aware of it, his image has been fixed indelibly within her.

During the last few miles before Thunder Bay, after the man has disappeared, after the car has returned to its preordained isolation, when the virtue, the rightness, of her mission should, according to design, bring comfort and strength, a strange thing begins to happen.

Whirling thought within thought extends beyond the window reflection, far beyond even the cold, dark earth. And she believes: *Something is wrong. This is not the way it goes. The latticework has been twisted. The man presumed; he happened when he shouldn't have.* Overhead the lights blaze as she hears other sounds, remembers echoed shouting in the upstairs apartment. *Her only living child*, she thinks, *I am twenty-three years from her, and even now she defaces the letters.* Outside, the lights of a small town appear like so many sparks, incredulous and scattered, flickering on the dark landscape. *Closer now*, she thinks, *Too close. Something has gone wrong. The design has warped and buckled and gnarled.*

With on her face an expression of profound, implacable sadness, she first focuses attention on the sign at the front of the car, NO SMOKING; then she notices the small, white sleeve buttons of her shirt. An arm is exposed in the stark light, and the red-brown rows of numinous lacerations. It seems to her very strange that she has not thought of the arm before.

While she studies the crusted marks, her right hand feels inside the purse, not for eyeglasses or lighter, but for an object enclosed within folded paper. The blade is new and clean and bright; she does not need to look at it. Her right hand acts independently, as though it had a life of its own. With an attitude of wonderment, she watches the exposed arm. She watches something sink beneath the skin and release the blood, thinking, *Clean. The pain is so clean.* And the bright red blood glides over her thumbnail. In that instant she believes she is not alone in the car, but her eyes can only discern the sign. The letters, red and clean against a white background, seem to contain a prophetic word, the summation of truth revealed. Then, as her fading, weary face continues to stare, the letters sort of blur at the edges, melting, burning, flowing like soft wax. Beyond the window an orange light is growing out of the flat, cold earth. The city approaches. It slides toward the train, ready to envelop and blind her. But the pain is faithful: For a time it abolishes all remorse, outrage, and terror. The smell of her own blood adheres to the air. And now the train's primitive voice, excessive and unrestrained, rises out of the shrinking darkness.

2

The hour is late and the walk is longer than she remembered.

After a while the myriad streets begin to run together as one street, splendid, inevitable, leading through a city that time has changed completely. Yet it does not matter to her that the city has changed. For Helen, everything of significance remains as it was twenty-three years before: suspended, somehow eternal. She goes on, walking away from the railroad station, unerring toward her destination, conveying a large and bulky suitcase across the immutable winter night.

Then the sleet begins; it stings her face and hands and legs. Next to her body, as a sort of protection, she holds her left arm, the one that, underneath the coat, is wrapped with strips of white cloth, awkwardly bandaged. Cold wind cleanses the vacant lots and the broken streets, whispering of reproach, warning of inescapable crisis. But she continues on, her purpose guided by years of watching and waiting for the revelation that is now at hand. *I have waited for twenty-three years*, she thinks, *And at last the hour is come.*

It is the wooden signboard, lighted by two small spotlights, that catches her attention. Beyond the sign are solemn gray walls, walls she has seen before. She can remember hurrying past this sprawl of buildings perhaps as many as a thousand times. The gray stone structure is, she believes, an integral part of the sequence of events that has brought her back to Thunder Bay with such an overriding urgency. But the lighted sign, with its careful hand lettering, is not known to her. It reads: Chapel Open for Meditation 8:00 A.M. to 10.00 P.M.

Memory waits, hovers in the thick darkness, until at last full recognition dawns, and she remembers it to be St. Ignatius' Church. The church stands at the center of a neighborhood with which she is quite familiar. Only a few blocks away lies her destination: the shapeless, sooted building where she grew to womanhood, the apartment where the mother yet lives in dead and bitter solitude. But still she waits, while memory continues, contemplating the small child who often stood on this same gray sidewalk, watching the priests and nuns in their silent black robes; watching too the children who wore uniforms (they were students at the parochial school); they were the children she was not allowed to play with. Her father disapproved of the uniforms and the school and the Church of Rome. He disapproved vocally and often spoke of dark excesses and whispered blasphemies.

This she remembers as she stands quite still, with her coat becoming ice-glazed, examining the small and vulnerable meditation chapel, which appears to be seeking shelter in one of the joints of the upswept limestone wall. As she waits there, she recalls her father's harsh-bitten words about the Catholic Church.

But when she moves, it is toward the chapel. It is as if her body already knows where it intends to go and she, following after, merely surrenders and steps through a set of carved doors into a dimly lighted entryway.

Intricate shadows edge down the walls and onto the cold stone floor. Shivering, Helen sees before her a second set of doors with a thin light glowing under and between them. In the entryway is an ornate marble font. She is thinking, *Holy water. The sign of the cross*, as she enters the chapel, and the double doors silently shut behind her.

Immediately visible is a statue of the Blessed Virgin, in front of which has been placed a wrought iron stand containing many small candles in red glass holders. Most of the candles are lighted. *For the dead*, she thinks, looking up at the sculptured stone, *It is the Mother of God.* Then she turns, moving slowly, like a person caught in some irresistible, macabre dance.

From the ceiling at the far end of the room a crucifix hangs; beneath it is a marble altar, which has been draped in purple. Helen walks partway down the aisle, stepping quite lightly on the floor that is worn, eroded, by the feet of many years. Then she stops and slides the large suitcase in between two pews. She sits down, leaning hard against the thick piece of wood that forms the armrest at the end of the pew.

Facing her is a lectern on which rests an open book. She thinks, *It is the Bible, the Holy Book,* and she yearns to go to it, to read from its open pages. But she will not move because she is in church, and because her father taught her how to behave in church (and also taught her about Jesus and the Bible after he realized it was up to him to lead her in upright and godly ways). "Helen," he would say, "you must learn that every tree that does not bear good fruit will be cut down and cast into the fire." He said it just like that, while she knelt on the rough wooden floor of the small apartment, she only seven years old at the time. But the mother would not kneel. She refused even to listen, saying that the Church had already robbed her of enough life and the father's austere Jesus was not going to rob her of any more.

Now, sitting in the chapel's fragrant warmth, with the sleet from her coat melting into harmless water droplets, Helen recalls another church, the community meeting hall that her father attended and helped build with his own calloused hands. There was a Bible there too, large and black and leather-bound; on Sunday the preacher would read from it, now and again holding up the open Bible for everyone to see. At the father's funeral the preacher read, "Whosoever believeth in me," while mother and daughter sat, stiff and gaunt, in the front row.

And now, more than twenty years later, the Bible is still open—Helen sees it there on the lectern. And she breathes the fragrance of incense that permeates the small chapel, thinking: *The book is a sign, part of the revelation. She who has refused, defaced, all of my letters, must now listen and watch and weep with me. The hour is at hand.*

Behind her are red-glowing votive candles. But there is something else behind her too. Listening, she can hear it: The double doors swing open, then close; footsteps sound, hesitating at the back of the chapel. Helen does not turn. She knows without looking that another now shares this space, breathes this air. Next she hears a different sound—like wood scraping on the stone floor, and a creaking. *Someone is kneeling by the candles*, she thinks, *Prayers for the dead, and a candle lighted.* She wants to turn around, but she does not, thinking, *This is part of the overall design*, believing, *It was meant for me to be in this holy place before I see her, before I see my mother.*

Murmured words rise and fall. Helen listens intently. Although she does not understand why or what, it occurs to her that perhaps some sort of miracle is taking place. She strains to hear the words, to eavesdrop on the other's prayer. "Our Father," she hears from the muffled voice. "Our Father," she repeats softly and completes the prayer in her mind. She thinks, *On this night a sign will be given*, while hearing, as the murmuring continues, "Blessed art thou among women." It is a female voice she hears; the voice is both young and old. Helen knows the prayer to be the rosary, and she smiles, thinking, *Beads on a string. Each action has been placed in a prescribed order.* Then the wood creaks again as the other stands up, her prayer complete.

Purpose moves through Helen's body. *There is still time*, she thinks, *It is like beads on a string, that's all; that's all.* Standing, she turns to see who it is that has prayed to Mary, the Mother of God. But what she sees causes her to take in a quick, a frightened breath.

It is not so much the face that shocks (the woman she beholds has kindness in her features); it is rather the eyes—they are fathomless, evasive, like those of a wild animal. The woman is dressed entirely in rags. Red hair stands out from her head like a terrific red halo. She looks young, younger than Helen, but there is a sad, frail weariness to her shoulders. "What?" she says. "What are you staring at?"

Helen does not answer. In the dim light she observes that the other's clothes sparkle, glisten, with particles of ice, thinking, *She walked here, as I did, walked here through the storm.*

In a voice quite wild, quite crazy, the woman suddenly says, "You think I don't know who you are? You think you can be anonymous with me? Well, you go to hell!" On her back she carries a canvas knapsack; she is holding two black plastic bags. And she squints a little, as though not seeing very well in the dimness. With one hand now she waves Helen from her sight. "Go on! I'd rather sleep on the sidewalk anyway, you self-righteous bag!" Beside her the votive lights burn.

At that moment the skin on Helen's neck stings as if it has been prodded by tiny needles.

The red-haired one's voice waxes and wanes. Then she makes a gesture indescribable, of desperation and leashed rage and something like fatigue. She says: "Hey, listen, give me a break. What I need is something to eat. Just some food. Look, I'm being honest with you. I've got to get something to eat or die. So how about it? You got spare change for me?" The woman wraps a scarf of tattered wool close around her neck and shuffles toward Helen, dragging the plastic bags behind her. As she nears, it is obvious that she wears on her feet only a large pair of men's slippers. "Look, I'm being straight with you," she says to Helen, who does not, cannot, move. "For God's sake, give me a break."

Helen knows she can say nothing. It is as if she has witnessed something so preemptive, so profoundly terrible, that speech has vanished from her. Eyes still on the other, she opens her purse and finds the wallet within.

The woman's dirty, outstretched hand clutches at the bills Helen offers. "God bless you," she says and steps back. "You're a kind and generous person. There aren't many like you in this world." Animal-like, she sidles down the aisle and toward the chapel doors, her voice remaining behind: "God bless you for it," she says.

Helen notices that the woman walks with a peculiar gait, as though one leg might be shorter than the other. Then the slippers cross the entryway and pass through the double doors, which whisper shut.

After the red-haired woman has left, the chapel seems remote and hollow and strange. For a time Helen waits, but the other does not reappear. Then, pulling the suitcase from between the pews and taking the handle once more in her right hand, she walks back down the aisle of the chapel to the double doors. Perhaps because of the lateness of the hour, or perhaps because she has traveled so far, the bag feels heavier, more burdensome than before.

At the stand of votive candles, she pauses to watch what is, for her, the holy fire of many prayers. Words, addressed neither to the candles nor to any living person, pass through her mind: *I wrote letters, you know. A new letter every week. And each of them was blackened, returned to me, her daughter. Yet it is I who will ask forgiveness tonight. Because the time is come for reconciliation.*

Helen steps outside into the sleeted air. She looks up and down the street, imagining, hoping even, that she will again see the limping, ragged woman. But only shadow and light are manifest on the empty street.

3

Freezing rain is everywhere, slanting across her path, transforming the familiar neighborhood into an all but incomprehensible series of streets and alleys. Once she mistakes a driveway for the road, and a dog barks loud from a darkened porch. Her heart pounding, Helen tries to walk faster, but patches of ice on the sidewalk threaten her balance. It is as if she has become again a child who is out too late, a child who is going to be punished for not getting home on time. She forgets to cross at corners and watch for traffic lights; several drivers honk at her, yelling curses into the frozen night.

She has forgotten about the chapel and the red-haired woman who uttered wild, dislocating words. She is thinking now only of the apartment building that must be very near indeed. There the mother waits, bitter and lonely in a third-floor flat, who at this hour might be heating water for tea, or maybe even gazing out a window at the selfsame winter night.

She walks on, recalling plaster walls and the rough wooden floor upon which she knelt each evening, as still as all fear, rocklike, and with her eyes tightly shut. After prayers she would sit in a straight-backed chair while the father read and talked, his dark-colored suit resembling the suit the preacher wore on Sundays. Then the father would look out into boundless space, the glory of his sanctification magnified beyond all thinking, all dreaming. "Oh, my poor vulnerable lamb," he would say, "the Devil is ready to swallow your soul if you do not turn to God. The Spirit of the Lord has enabled me to bear witness, to tell you of the love of Jesus and the danger you are in. How it grieves me to know that your own mother has left you defenseless against Satan; how it grieves me."

Walking, she remembers the father, and her right arm aches from the burden of the large suitcase. But she does not put the bag down, nor rest, nor catch her breath. A primitive, indomitable urgency tracks her, hounds her like a hungry animal as she retraces the steps of a thin, unbearable grief-journey already twenty-three years long.

She tightens her grip on the handle of the suitcase. Looking up from the icy path, she sees, straight ahead and across one final street, the solitary, brick apartment building, which rises out of the pavement like some lethargic, dark specter. She crosses the street, thinking, *Tonight. Tonight the sin will be expiated.* The outer door is locked, but when she rattles the handle, she hears a loud buzz and the door latch springs open. Helen enters.

For several seconds she half-shuts her eyes against the outrageous glare of an overhead light. Then a sick feeling intrudes upon her. It seems almost as if she has arrived at an alien place. The lobby has been reshaped, disfigured: Only in outline is it the same. Slowly she examines the stained plaster walls, sensing a dull, obliterating violence everywhere around her.

"Yes?" The voice emanates from a corner of the room; it belongs to a man who sits at a desk behind a long wooden counter, on top of which has been taped a strand of blinking, multicolored lights. The garish lights make the man's features look eerie, not human. "How may I help you?" he says. On the desktop is an open magazine; there are full-color pictures of nudes on the visible pages.

"What's going on?" she asks. "What happened to the lobby?" The echo of her own words returns from the stained plaster walls.

"Just the same old lobby," he says. "Do you want a room, is that it?" His voice sounds wary; it is almost as though she is unwelcome, strange. And the string of red-blue-green lights keeps blinking and blinking like a cheap neon sign.

"A room?" she says. "Why would I want a room?"

The man stands up behind the desk. "This is a hotel, lady. Didn't you see the sign?"

For the first time since she has entered the building, Helen puts the suitcase down. She tenses against the unquiet trembling that has taken hold of her. "How can this be a hotel? I have come here to see my mother—Mrs. Roth. She lives in Apartment 3C."

"Mrs. who?" The voice now seems to come from a shadow-realm.

"Mrs. Roth; Mary Roth in 3C. She is my mother."

"Wait a minute," he says, and turns away.

As the string of lights shifts from color to color, and the walls resound with the memory of shouting and that other Christmas (never forgotten, yet remembered always without tears), Helen waits. She waits in disbelieving quiet because she knows that two flights up and three doors past the staircase is the apartment where the mother lives. The man behind the counter she has begun to regard as a sort of mythic doorkeeper, a spirit guide who will soon usher her back to the known world.

Across the dead silence come words she cannot quite hear: The man is talking on the telephone. But he has turned his back—as if, for now, to conceal from her the truth. On the wall behind him hangs a clock with a broken glass face. *Time is dying*, Helen thinks, *Minutes are falling between the cracks in the universe.*

He hangs up the phone and looks at her again, though she refuses in her heart to believe what his eyes tell her before ever the words speak it. "I'm sorry, lady. Since they made this building into a hotel, there hasn't even been an Apartment 3C. And there isn't anyone named Mary Roth living here." He is no longer wary; his voice is downcast. "Nor do I have a record of any tenant named Roth who used to live here—not as far back as these files go." He waits; it is as though he expects her immediately to pick up the suitcase and leave, simply leave. "What I'm trying to say is: Your mother's not here. I'm sorry."

Helen stiffens. She says, "But that's not possible. I have written to her at this address." She stands now in the attitude of one who has been betrayed, recalling the white envelopes she has saved, each one blackened, refused and then returned. "I'll show you," she says, reaching for the handle of the suitcase, "I'll show you, that's all. It is Apartment 3C."

Yet before her winter-cold fingers can lift the bulky leather suitcase, the man says: "Wait, lady. Don't go upstairs. This here's no place for you to go wandering around. Your mother's not here. I even called the owner of the building, late as it is.

He remembers back some fifteen years. Honest, your mother's not here."

Now it is as though she has entered a gray limbo; a tiny spiral of fear thickens and flares within her mind, shaping at last into a strange, wordless picture. She watches herself running without ever her feet touching the earth, without tiring or stopping, floating like the cold night wind, running back home. Yet in the picture, that is all there is: the running. She does not ever arrive.

4

When the grayness clears from Helen's eyes, the hotel man is telling her that she has fainted, blacked out, right there in the lobby. He helps her up and hands her a mug of coffee with whiskey in it.

At that moment she feels like a person who, while climbing a cliff, has suddenly let go of the safety rope and now can sense the shortening of space and distance beneath her: falling, fading, vanishing into an incomprehensible, soundless vacuum. Her hands ache, and she realizes she has been clenching against an invisible encroachment of despair, the dissolving in fire and smoke of her hope, and yes, of the immortality of it, the cleansing forgiveness, which rises eternal above even the grave's molded end. As if from somewhere far away, she can hear the sound of the man's voice (talking again on the telephone, perhaps), but she does not try to listen to the words.

Upon returning, he says, "It's as much as my job is worth," saying it as if she, without knowing, has placed a demand on his life. She does not answer. She waits in dreamlike suspension until he continues. "I went and called the owner back. He doesn't like being bothered at night for anything less than a fire or a busted pipe—so it's not that he's in the best of moods. But he did say he's been thinking about it, and maybe he does remember a Mrs. Roth who lived here, and it was Mission Street where she probably moved to. Most of them that got tossed out when this place became a hotel ended up there—Mission Street near Market."

The man asks Helen several times if she is sure she is all right. Then he telephones for a cab, insisting that she must take a taxicab downtown.

"Not fit for a dog to be out on a night like this," he says from the entrance of the hotel, as he watches her get into the hired car. "It's that wind from off the bay." And Helen watches his face recede as she is conveyed, carried weary away from the desolate rubble of her expectations.

The cab lets her out at the intersection of Mission and Market streets. Stepping out onto the icy pavement, she hears the clock in the tower of the railroad station sound. She pauses to count the chimes. *Ten o'clock*, she thinks, taking in a single breath, and thinking too: *She has moved to Mission Street. Here I*

*will find her—the mother who was dispossessed, exiled
from her own home. Here at last I will find her.*

The city is rank with poverty; the streets are cold
and narrow and loud. Loud, drunken voices can be
heard, loud through the thin walls, and somewhere
in the darkness, footsteps hasten down a long fire
escape. Undaunted, she walks on, peering hard into
lighted shop windows, as if expecting her mother
to appear there in tableau, all motionless and impervious to time. Muscles aching, she is still carrying
the large suitcase, moving slowly among all the gar-
bage cans and the grime and the desolate, mortal
buildings. And she is thinking: *It is the right thing to
do. I am fifty years old. She must weep with me now for
all that has gone before.*

She enters an apartment building and knocks repeatedly on a door that is marked, MANAGER. Within
the apartment she can hear the sound of someone's
cramped, hidden progress toward her knocking.
Then the door opens, revealing an older woman,
tall and gaunt, with a face that is absolutely calm,
and just raising her voice enough to be heard.
"Yeah?" she says.

"I am looking for Mary Roth," Helen says.

"Mary Roth, . . ." the woman says.

"I thought she might live in this building," Helen
says. "She moved to Mission Street."

The gaunt woman starts to shut the door. "It's a
long street, daughter," she says.

"Does she live here?" Helen says. "That's all I'm asking. Does she?"

The sound that follows is a sharp and final click of the door latch. "Never heard of her," the woman's voice says through the door.

After that, Helen grows more methodical in her approach, asking at each building, clinging, like someone who is drowning, to the ephemeral hope promised by each new encounter. *This one will know her. It is not ended. It cannot be ended*, she thinks. But in none of the apartment buildings can the mother be found; no one recognizes the name Mary Roth; not a single person can recall the woman that Helen describes. Each new door shuts upon her with brutal, incisive finality.

In desperation, she begins to ask passersby, "Have you seen my mother?" forgetting sometimes even to say who her mother is, or to explain why she is searching for her here on Mission Street. As she goes on, she forgets more and more. Most of the people she asks merely stare at her, walking past without even curiosity. It is as if the streets have lost any and every capacity for caring, for surprise, for vulnerability.

Yet one there is who stops, one who listens. He wears a woolen cap and his eyes are the eyes of youth, of a young man. "You're out of breath, ma'am," he says. "Take your time. I can't make out what you are saying."

Speaking more slowly, encouraged by his kindness, Helen tells the story with exaggerated care, as though in a prolonged and unbroken instant of tremendous effort she might finally be able to make someone understand. Her listener nods occasionally. When the story is finished, she says, "Please help me. Do you know where my mother lives?"

But the young man does not know. "Are you sure she lives anywhere?" he says.

"Why, of course I am sure," Helen says. "She is not dead—she is not dead!"

Again the young man starts to speak, but then he checks himself as if his thoughts suddenly have altered course. He looks sad. "It's possible that she might live on the street, you know," he says.

"What do you mean?" she says.

"Well," he says, "it sounds like your mother's pretty old. And lots of old folks these days can't afford even a single room."

"Oh," Helen says. She goes silent.

And she believes that the young man will soon leave, thinking, *His soul shrinks from human limitation. He knows he can do nothing, be nothing, that will help*, while she is saying, "But if my mother is on the street, how will I be able to find her?"

The young man adjusts the woolen cap on his head. "I don't know," he says. "Except that maybe one of the street people around here might know her, might know if she's one of them." Then, before she can question him further, he walks off, going down the street with lowered head and hunched shoulders.

It is as though the world has grown older while they talked. Slowed by exhaustion and the heavy suitcase, Helen does not permit herself to consider what the young man has said, nor does she think anymore about all the closed doors in the apartment houses. She becomes part of the street, walking in an endless track, walking alone into the heart of the unknown. She does not cease walking until the clock at the railroad station chimes another hour into existence.

The clock seems to be closer than when she first heard it. With the suitcase placed on the sidewalk next to her, Helen stands staring down the narrow length of Mission Street. Buildings have further darkened; very few windows show light from within.

While she is wondering what she will do next, where she will go, there is a shifting of shadows. Slowly the street's coarse obscurity gives birth to a human figure that limps as if one leg were shorter than the other. The face of the woman approaching has a blank and barren appearance, and when the ragged outline nears, Helen glimpses a halo of red hair under the cold, thin glow of the street lamp. "I know you," she says. "You were at the church."

The red-haired woman stops; her eyes communicate a kind of wary incomprehension. "Just who are you speaking to?"

"I saw you earlier at the church," Helen says. "Don't you remember?" She says it quickly, for fear the wraithlike woman might vanish into the darkness.

"At the church?" the woman says, shrugging her rag-covered shoulders. "Maybe so. This time of year especially, I pray. Last week there was a man grabbed me and tried to rape me. I prayed then; I prayed loud. He ran away like he was on fire." Her voice echoes across the empty night. Then she appears to forget about Helen. She commences shuffling along the sidewalk again, the black plastic bags dragging behind her, her tired eyes searching the shadows for danger or for food.

"Wait," Helen says, "don't go yet."

The woman turns. "Have you got change for me?" she says. Her voice becomes automatic, remote. "I sure could use some change."

"Help me," Helen says. "I need your help."

The other pulls the plastic bags closer to herself with an air of someone who is afraid she is about to be robbed. "How?" she says. "No one asks me for nothing. Leave me alone!" She stands holding the knapsack and plastic bags as if they were spoils of war.

"It's my mother," Helen says. "I've got to find her."

Shivering, the red-haired woman moves her feet back and forth in the large slippers. A peculiar slyness enters her features, and she says, "Sure . . . I

124

knew it when I first seen you. When I first seen you, I said to myself, 'That there lady, she is looking for someone, maybe even her mother.' "

Helen breathes in and out. An extraordinary weariness has taken possession of her. "Please," she says, "I have to find her tonight."

"Yes, of course you do." The woman nods and the halo of red hair catches the lamplight.

"Her name is Mary Roth. Do you know her? Do you know where she is?" Helen pauses, waits for a reply. But the other says nothing, seems almost to have fallen asleep standing up. "They told me at the apartment house that she had moved to Mission Street," Helen says. "And a man I met said she might be living on the street."

Beneath layers of scarves and coats the red-haired woman continues to shiver. "I've got to find a bed tonight," she says to herself. "I swear I do."

For a time the frozen world remains suspended. On the street no other human beings are evident, and the loud, drunken voices have quieted. All that Helen can hear now is her own breathing. The night has moved beyond reasonableness, beyond outrage even. Helen's hands and feet are completely numb. She says again: "Her name is Mary Roth. Do you know her?"

"Mary . . . Roth," the woman says, as if understanding the name for the first time. "Old Mary, that would be. Sure, I know Old Mary."

"You do know her?"

"That's what I said, ain't it?"

"You're certain her name is Mary Roth?"

Like plumage on a bird, the rags rearrange themselves. The woman's face reflects a vague taking of offense. "Look," she says, "you want to find her, or not?"

"I do, yes. I want to find her," Helen says, believing now with a fierce certainty. "Where is my mother?"

So, leaving Mission Street, the two set out together, traveling like Magi on a singular midnight quest. The red-haired woman talks without ceasing. Again and again she stretches her arms over the desolate street in a strange gesture of blessing or of curse.

Nor can Helen understand much of what the woman says—the flow of words is primitive, fabulous, hidden—but it seems that they are approaching some sort of salvation. The other's gestures grow wilder, and the large slippers shuffle ever more quickly along a path Helen does not recognize. *It has been foreordained; it is meant to be,* Helen thinks, her heart excited, rushing, within her.

The streets no longer seem deserted. Everywhere Helen can feel distinct, yet invisible movement. They turn a corner and she sees the gleam of living fire: On the sidewalk stands a barrel from which the flames arise. Around the slender outpouring of heat has gathered a circle of gray, random people who resemble otherworldly figures chanting before a silent god.

The red-haired woman does not hesitate, hurries forward, running almost. Beyond the fire are more lights, more people; here several streets come together. Helen looks across the intersection, catches sight of the woman as she turns and disappears through an arched doorway. Helen's feet move automatically. With effort she pulls each breath from the chill air, thinking, *I will not let her get away, I will not.*

Hurrying through the doorway where the woman disappeared, Helen suddenly realizes that she has entered the Thunder Bay Railroad Station. Only a few hours before did she carry the leather suitcase from this same station into the night, passing under the tower clock that even now is chiming once, announcing the demise of another thirty minutes of human time.

Inside the station, every sound is amplified by the high ceiling and the cold, undecorated walls. Helen, her eyes round and fearful, searches for the red-haired woman amid the benches, on which are sitting late-night travelers, some of whom appear quite tired and apathetic, while others exude a sort of nostalgic excitement. She notices that at the center of the room there stands a tall evergreen tree, its branches laden with tiny white lights. The tree seems to be saying something, speaking some universal truth. For an instant Helen believes she understands, she knows, what is being said, but the thought leaves her when she glimpses, across the station, a halo of red hair.

Near the gate to an eastbound train, the ragged woman waits. The familiar plastic bags are clumped at her feet like mute worshipers; everywhere around now is a serene, ethereal hush.

"Where is she?" Helen says, approaching. "Where is my mother?"

"Oh, she's here," the woman says. "Don't you worry none. Old Mary is always around here."

"Show me," Helen says.

"But maybe she don't want to see you." The woman tilts her head to the side. "You ever think of that?"

"You're stalling," Helen says. "I don't believe you know where she is!" In a distracted, edgeless tone, she says, "It has been twenty-three years. . . ." The loudspeaker echoes the name of a city, a time, and a gate number. The sound makes Helen frown. *It doesn't go like this*, she thinks, *This is not the way it goes*. She looks around the room, scrutinizing every bench, every corner. She believes that she must surely find her mother among those who are waiting, or perhaps among those who are moving quickly along in response to the echoing, eternal voice of the loudspeaker. But the people who pass by merely stare at her and look away.

"I wasn't going to tell you," the ragged woman says, reclaiming Helen's attention, "but your mother ain't been well lately. She's been kind of sick."

"You find her," Helen's voice is tense, abrupt. "You find her right now."

The red-haired woman appears to be weighing something in her heart. Then she says, "I guess a daughter has the right. I oughtn't come between kinfolk." The plastic bags are again hoisted; the slippers whisper across the station floor. Looking back at Helen, the woman enters the gate near which they have been standing. "This train ain't due to board for another half hour," she says. "Old Mary's got herself a place to rest down here, I'll warrant."

Helen carries the bulky suitcase and follows like a disciple. They pass into a cool, dusty tunnel, which is lighted by fluorescent rods that are strung along the ceiling like Christmas lights. The sound of their footsteps collides with the tunnel's walls, returning all amplified and distorted. It does not seem to Helen that any living thing could survive in this place. The tunnel ends at another tunnel that is perpendicular to the first and larger; within it stands a vacant train. The windows of the train's segmented body are quite dark. It looks almost as if it has been blinded by some capricious god, blinded and left in solitude to die.

Out of the dimness comes coughing. The red-haired woman moves toward the sound.

Thick gloom frightens: Helen wants to run away, to escape, like all the people who have hurried past her tonight. Something determinative waits in the place where the coughing is, and she is not sure she has the strength or the courage to face it. "I can't," she says suddenly, but the cavernous tunnel swallows the words.

Before she can say further, they stop. In front of them, huddled on the floor, coughing, is an old woman, her body curled like a fetus and wedged into a small alcove. The skin of the woman's hands stretches tight over brittle, angular bones; her face is invisible, buried in the folds of a thin shawl; all that can be seen of her head are a few strands of white hair.

Helen stands trembling, looking at the woman. "Dear God," she says, "is this really my mother?"

A head raises from the shawl, revealing a face that bears all the furrows and creases of advanced age. Helen kneels next to the woman, who immediately tries to move away. "Get away from me!" she says. "I've been bothered enough for one night. Just let me stay here for a while. At least till the train is called."

"Mother," Helen says, tears forming in her eyes.

The woman stops moving and stares at Helen. "What?" she asks. "What did you say?"

"I've come to you, Mother—after twenty-three years. You must not refuse to see me now, here, in the train station." Helen's voice is quiet, amazed, as she continues to kneel, thinking, *The features are so different from what I remember. She looks so different.*

"I ain't your mother," the woman says.

A few feet away, leaning against the wall, the red-haired woman stands, humming to herself, a tired, indifferent sentinel. And it occurs to Helen that maybe the other remains nearby because she is playing a part, a part that has not yet ended.

Again a cough takes hold of the ancient woman; it ravages the fragile body before at last releasing her. *Why, she is dying*, Helen thinks, the thought sudden, desolate. She puts her hands on the woman's shoulders as if to shield her from the onrush of death.

"What are you doing?" the woman says.

Helen says, "You need help."

"Now, don't go worrying about Old Mary," the woman says. "This cough ain't killed me yet."

"Please don't hate me," Helen says.

"Hate you?" the old woman says, pulling the shawl closer to her body. "I don't hate no one at all, not even the cops or the station guards. They only do what they have to do." She watches Helen for several seconds, her eyes vague, unfocused. "Do I know you?"

"Yes," Helen says. "I'm your daughter, your only living child."

Pursing her lips, the woman says, "No, not my daughter." Her eyes are a dull mud color; they resemble oil lanterns that have dimmed from lack of fuel. "Though I remember taking care of a child once. It was very long ago. Are you that child?"

"Yes," Helen says. "I am Helen."

The old woman goes quiet; her body relaxes and she begins to rock back and forth. Then she says, "I remember. Yes, I remember. But . . . I thought it was a little boy I took care of." Her chest rises and falls with the tentativeness of a spiderweb fluttering in the spring wind.

Upon Helen's heart is a heaviness that does not yet know itself to be grief, inarticulate desiccated grief. "You had three sons," she says in a thick voice. "Three little boys. All of them died as infants. I was the last born; I am the only child who survived."

"Not me; you're thinking of somebody else," the woman says, lowering her head as in prayer, while Helen tries to reconcile the memory of shouted words and running footsteps with the reality that is huddled before her on the cold, ghostly floor, thinking, *She is so old, I would never have recognized her*, yet thinking, *It was the right thing to do, to come here.* Next she senses the old woman recede, drift away sort of, toward another existence. Grasping the frail arm, she says, "Oh, Mother, don't leave me!"

The woman shakes her head. "Did I fall asleep?" she asks. "A fine thing. Someone comes to see me, someone who isn't trying to move me to elsewhere, and I fall asleep." She takes Helen's hand in her shrunken fingers, stares at it with childlike wonder. She turns the hand over, examining the palm as might a fortuneteller at the carnival.

Helen tries to pull away, tries to hide the under-side of the wrist with its red-brown scars, its vestiges of self-inflicted punishment. But the old woman clings to her hand with surprising strength. She looks closely at the scars. "You're hurt," she says.

And Helen tries to speak, but the words do not find expression. In that underground place, cut off from everything she has ever known, with around her only the cold and empty tunnel, every expla-nation, every justification, simply disappears like mist. She allows her hand to remain in the woman's grasp.

"You done it to yourself," the other says. Her dark eyes are sad, urgent.

"No," Helen says. "No, I didn't—"

"Yes," the woman says; she talks rapidly, as though trying to forestall an impending menace. "It was you that did the cutting, nobody else. Just like my friend Winifred Page, you are. Using pain to hide the pain of it, the raw reality of it." Her voice weakens, drops in volume. Helen grips the woman's hand as if to transfer life to her whose eyes now seem to be searching the shadows at the end of the tunnel. "You ain't the only one ever done it, you know. Winifred done it, too."

Helen says, "I don't understand—"

"She had scars like yours. She was young and desperate. Alone on her pilgrimage through the darkness. The pain inside of her got so bad, she couldn't even leave her room. Just sat all day in a

133

chair and stared. Just sat there staring until it was time to go to bed again. She had scars like yours." The words diminish, cease. The old woman's breath rattles within her chest, a rattle that soon grows into more coughing.

Helen's face is wet with tears. "I can't stop doing it," she says. "I can't."

When she is clear of the coughing, the woman says, "You can stop. You've got to. There are other ways to live with the pain. Not to make it go away. To live with it." Again Helen tries to draw back her hand, but the woman's fingers are as tight as death.

"I'm afraid," Helen says, watching the other's dim eyes flicker.

"I know, child," the woman says. "I know. But you've got to stop hurting yourself. If not for you, then for me. I can't stand it." Minutes pass. In the old woman's face Helen sees mystery struggling with mystery.

"What about Winifred Page?" Helen says softly. "Whatever happened to her?"

"She finally died from it," the woman says. "She never could let go of the past. And the past, it just rotted her from the inside out."

"I . . . I'm sorry," Helen says.

"Yes," the woman says. "So am I." The fingers unclasp, release Helen's hand. "That's why I can't stand it for you to go on hurting yourself. Not that life is easy, God knows. It ain't easy or sensible or anything like that. But it's life. Even for folks like me who are on the street, it's life." Her voice subsides, ceases.

The tunnel above them looms like the ceiling of a Gothic cathedral. Cold permeates Helen's body. Pondering the other's words, she stares at the cold, gray walls and the ceiling. For a moment it is as if she has forgotten where she is. Nearby, all silent and impervious to the passing of time, stands the vacant, blind train. *Soon this train will be traveling from here*, Helen thinks, *Soon it will be absorbed into the future, leaving the past behind*. Against the tunnel wall leans the red-haired woman. She appears to be asleep.

Silence increases. Kneeling, Helen waits for the old woman's voice to resume, hungry for the strange, unexpected words. *It can't be true that she has nothing more to say*, she thinks, looking at the now-closed eyelids as if from an extraordinary distance. But the stillness remains intact. And, as the earth continues shifting on its axis, while stars go on living and dying in the infinity of space, a new awareness begins to unfold within Helen. It is as though the woman is still speaking to her, speaking without words, and Helen knowing, realizing, that her mother never stopped loving her, that the shouting and cursing of twenty-three years past is not a final judgment. Remembered words crumble now like the fragile remains of burned paper. Now also she realizes the truth about the letters.

Turning, she pulls the heavy suitcase toward her, opens it, and allows the lid to flop back. Next she

135

studies the interior where are arranged several par-
cels of envelopes in neat rows, each parcel tied with
a wide black ribbon. The case contains no clothing.
It contains nothing but the envelopes. Helen selects
one from a ribbon-tied parcel. Like each of the others, it bears her mother's name and address; a heavy
black line has been marked across the face of it; penciled there, too, is the word *Refused*. Holding the
envelope between her hands, she seems to see the
writing for the first time. "Why, look at this!" she
says to the woman whose eyes remain shut, whose
chest no longer makes even the slightest movement.

Yet it is the red-haired one who speaks. "Old
Mary's dead," she says. She has moved away from
the wall and now is standing above Helen and the
open suitcase. Upon herself she makes the sign of
the cross, saying, "Her soul has escaped even as a
bird out of the snare of the fowler. She's gone home
at last."

"No," Helen says, kneeling in the half-light, leaning over the huddled figure, feeling the coldness of
the ancient, transparent hands. "No, she's not dead;
she's sleeping, that's all."

"What you are looking at is mortal death, not
sleep," the woman says. "She died peaceful. Her face
looks easier than I have seen it."

"She can't be dead," Helen says.

"It done her good to see you," the woman says,
bending and looking at the envelopes in Helen's suitcase. "Say, what's that you've got?"

Then, although memory can still hear the shouting, feel the hard stairs under her feet, Helen knows she is no longer afraid. She knows that the voices and the running no longer have full power over her; they will never again become the same pulsing, deceitful nightmares. "It's a suitcase full of old letters," she says, while in her mind she adds, *Unmailed letters.*

"Written to your mother?"

"Yes. To my mother."

"How come they ain't got stamps?"

In her thoughts all the words Helen ever wished to speak begin to form. She is beside herself with words; they come too fast for her to utter. The woman who is lying so still, so eternal, before her has managed somehow to slip away, floating on the ebb of the River, taking with her all the fear and remorse and hatred.

The ragged woman's voice continues. "I figure it's mighty weird—writing all those letters to someone and then not mailing them."

"She didn't refuse them," Helen says. "She didn't. It was I who did not mail them." Her voice sounds weak, grateful, like that of someone who has just been rescued from a deep well.

"Too weird for me," the woman says, starting to walk away. "If I had nice clothes like yours, that's what I'd put in my suitcase, not some old letters."

"Wait," Helen says. "Where are you going?"

"She's dead. Ain't no use staying around."

"But what will happen to her?"

137

The red-haired woman pauses. "Same as would happen if it was me—nothing. When the train is boarded, somebody's sure to find her. She'll be taken to the morgue with no identification, no address, no name. That's about it."

"She's my mother!"

"You tell them that, then. And you bury her. As for me, I don't like to hang around where the cops are gonna be showing up. I'm an undesirable, like Old Mary. So, ashes to ashes and dust to dust." Down the tunnel the halo of red hair moves. Only the woman's voice reaches back through the dimness. "We brought nothing in with us, and it's for sure we carry nothing out. The Lord gives; the Lord takes away."

Helen watches her who is still dragging two black plastic bags turn and disappear under a sign that says EXIT. And while she is watching, the loudspeaker begins. It rings deep into the heart of the tunnel, filling the echoing gloom with its voice. *They're announcing this very train*, Helen thinks and stands up, legs stiff. The old woman's body looks insubstantial, transformed, as if the molecules have been rearranged into some other entity altogether. Helen bows her head, thinking, *I must decide. I must decide what to do next.*

Then, walking from the tunnel, she passes under the Exit sign without giving thought either to the sign or to the passengers who now make their way toward her, headed for the outward-bound train.

5

The station has thinned of people. A janitor cleans the floor with languorous sweeps of a gray rag mop. Helen finds herself walking among the nearly empty benches, alone but not solitary. No longer burdened by the heavy suitcase, she makes her way easily across the room. Then she stops. Directly ahead are standing two uniformed police officers. Even though they seem to be in conversation, their eyes survey the room with all the watchfulness of life-guards. It occurs to her that she might speak to them, but something prevents her. *Not yet*, she thinks, *There is more, more that I must do before telling*.

She sits down on one of the wooden benches. In her lap she folds her hands, as if she were in church waiting for the minister to read the holy Word: a child again, except that she no longer feels so lost and afraid. *Something has been relinquished*, she thinks, *and something has been gained*. Then she sees the tall evergreen tree that is decorated with tiny white lights. She believes the tree holds a special significance for her, though at the moment she cannot think what it might be. Then her notice is caught by people moving fast toward the gate from which she has just come. The two police officers are with a man who looks frightened, agitated. Helen thinks, *They are going to take care of my mother. They will know what to do*, remembering the letters that are in the suitcase next to the woman's body—envelopes tied with ribbon, each bearing the mother's name and address. *The letters will be a sign to these strangers who even now are approaching her*, Helen thinks, *She will have a name, an identity.*

But, as she waits (without yet knowing what she is waiting for), another train is announced. And among the travelers advancing toward the gate she believes she sees a familiar face—that of the man who rode with her on the train to Thunder Bay. Squinting, Helen stands and attempts to better focus her eyes on him who makes his way across the station without speed or angularity. Yet she cannot be sure it is the same man, and soon the figure disappears through a gate. *He was right*, she thinks, *It did not turn out the way I believed it would. Revelation came, but it was not the revelation that I expected.*

Her vision blurring, she looks away from where, only a moment ago, the man was. She feels the earth pause, hesitate, while memories and pain swirl wildly, threatening to subsume her again. And she thinks, *The pain is coming back. What will I do?* Struggling against profound, intolerant panic, she holds her purse close, while standing rigid and immobile, knowing that in the purse is something she can use against the fear. There, enfolded in paper, is the stainless steel blade. This she knows. Yet, before her mind can make anything of the knowledge, the moment which she has been awaiting arrives. *There is more I must do*, she thinks, *Now it is time*. Without hesitation, she searches the purse, rummaging past the eyeglasses case and the lighter until she finds the folded paper. Then she walks over to a wastebasket with a swinging lid, and into this she drops the blade. A new wave .of panic boils around Helen when she sees it fall out of sight. She thinks, *I can't. I'm not strong enough*. But, as the blade drops soundlessly into the unseen space below, and the lid swings back into place, she hears herself saying, "I will not die like Winifred Page."

From a distance there comes the sound of a small bell (although Helen believes she has been hearing it all along). He wears a Salvation Army uniform, the one who rings the bell unceasingly and smiles at passersby. "Oh," she says, "can it really be Christmastime?"

No one answers; none of the people around her appears to have heard the question. But it does not matter to her that no one speaks. She stands listening to the bell, seeing the tall and fragrant Christmas tree at the center of the station, the lights of the tree resembling hundreds of votive candles with delicate flames rising into an immense and glorious sky. She stands there, breathing the clean pine smell, waiting, watching. A station door has been opened by the police in order to allow passage of a stretcher to a waiting ambulance. Outside, the temperature has dropped, and now through the open door, the wind off the bay is entering the nearly empty station, rushing and pouring across the floor unopposed, with terrific, sibilant force.

Unconsciously she reaches for the bulky suitcase. Then, remembering, she straightens and walks over to the janitor who is still mopping the floor. "When will it be Christmas?" she asks.

Startled, the man looks up. "Christmas?" he says. "In a couple minutes it's going to be Christmas Eve." He points to his watch.

"For heaven's sake," Helen says.

It is as if she has suddenly found herself at the edge of creation, in a place where history has not been written and the design of life is only in process of formation. The wind whirls fast and smooth; yet on the edges of it, hidden within it, she can hear another sound, a voice uncontrollable, fierce, proud. At first she believes that what she hears is a dog randomly raising its cry of mournful complaint. Soon, however, she realizes that the sound is much wilder than that; it overflows with savage passion, with all-embracing sorrow. The cry upon the wind remembers every heartbreak, calls out even to the smallest of creatures; it is a lament that comes from beyond the clouds and the thick darkness. More than anything on earth, it resembles the howl of a gray timber wolf.

While Helen waits, alive, baggageless, and precariously free, the wolflike wind howls and howls. And the night trains move smoothly out from beneath the station, moving silent and free, traveling toward the clean, transcendent chill of the approaching dawn.

DAILY
OFFICE

THE PRELUDE

L. Grace and peace be unto you.

C. From God our Father and the Lord Jesus Christ.

L. Amen.

C. Amen.

THE ACT OF CONFESSION

L. Let us stand as a broken people before the Mystery that sustains us all. We have been called to freedom, but we have found the demand too great, the anxiety too painful. We have returned to comfortable illusion. We are possessed by the demonic.

C. O Lord of all that is, we confess that we have created the chaos of our time. We repeatedly protect ourselves from the cries of the anguished. We persist in ravaging our natural and human resources. Amen.

145

L. Amen.

L. Forgive us this hatred of self, this alienation, this idolatry.

C. Pardon our readiness to hold others accountable for history, and our unreadiness to make the hard decisions required in time and space. Amen.

L. Amen.

L. Let us arise to create a new day. Each of us is free to live, free to decide. The past is approved; the future is open. We are accepted as we are— the broken, sinful, and forgiven people of God.

C. By this word we are enabled to embrace the possibility of our lives. Amen.

L. Amen.

THE ACT OF PROCLAMATION

L. I call upon us to stand present to our forebear Isaiah as he speaks:

> Then flew one of the seraphim to me, having in his hand a burning coal which he had

taken with tongs from the altar. And he touched my mouth, and said: "Behold this has touched your lips; your guilt is taken away, and your sin forgiven." And I heard the voice of the Lord saying, "Whom shall I send and who will go for us?" Then I said, "Here am I! Send me."

C. This is our passover, the night on which we are delivered. Amen.

L. Amen.

L. Stand present also to the gospel as proclaimed by Paul:

> Our old being has been put to death with Christ on his cross, in order that the power of the sinful self might be destroyed, so that we should no longer be the slaves of sin.

C. We testify that God raised Jesus Christ from the dead. For as in Adam all die, so in Christ shall all be made alive. Amen.

L. Amen.

L. Eternal Father, we give thanks for the unique and unrepeatable nature of history.

C. We give thanks especially for those events that bring questions to all our answers. Amen.

L. Amen.

L. We give thanks for the whole of creation. By the power of God, we rejoice in everything that is.

C. O Holy One, we rehearse the paradox that our decisions validate or invalidate all that has gone before, and make possible or impossible all that is yet to come. Amen.

L. Amen.

THE ACT OF OFFERING

L. O Lord of history, we lift up our brokenness as an offering to you.

C. We pray for those in sorrow, those in poverty, those in prison; for people suffering in body, mind, or spirit. We pray for the unwanted of creation, the discards of society. We remember particularly our own unworthiness. Amen.

L. Amen.

L. Enable us, O Giver of life, to stand open to those parts of ourselves we call other people. For there is no distinction; all have sinned and fall short of the glory of God. We are justified by grace as a gift, through the redemption which is in Christ Jesus.

C. Give us the courage to say yes to life. Amen.

L. Amen.

L. Turn us again, O God of Hosts.

C. Turn us again, O Lord.

L. The Christ-event is present to us.

C. Through him we have obtained access to this grace in which we stand, and we rejoice in our hope of sharing the glory of God. Amen.

L. Amen.

L. Once again we dedicate ourselves to a journey that leads to the cross. We present ourselves before God on behalf of all creation.

C. We renounce the illusion that life is about security. We cast out the demon that says human beings are expendable. Amen.

L. Amen.

L. Let us embrace a life-style that sees meaning in discipline and freedom in obedience.

C. Let us be steadfast in love, abounding in the work of the Lord, knowing that in the Lord our labor is not in vain. Amen.

L. Amen.

THE BENEDICTION

L. The grace of our Lord Jesus Christ, the love of God, and the fellowship of the Holy Spirit be with us all evermore. Amen.

C. Amen.

BRADY

It is on the bus that the idea of going to a funeral comes to me.

I am sitting in the back, in the smoking section, between the window and a woman who is wearing a hairnet. The woman got on at Altavista. Hauling a couple of huge shopping bags, and with a face resigned to fighting nothing but losing battles, she asked if the seat next to mine was taken, and that while she was in the very act of lowering herself into it. She seemed perplexed, dwarfed, by the experience of traveling out beyond the town and into the open countryside, kind of staring ahead of herself as the bus rolled on through fields obscured by patches of tentative early mist.

Now that we are about half an hour from Springfield, she is talking to me nonstop, as though the city's nearness has pumped new life into her or something. And I am trying to read a copy of the Springfield newspaper that I found upon boarding the bus in Gretna, which is the town where I've lived since birth. Gretna isn't much of a town. It doesn't have a daily paper; there's just this eight-page publication that comes out every week or so, all filled with pictures of children having birthday parties and of couples who've been married a real long time. It depresses me to read the Gretna paper. Someday I am going to live in a place that's big enough for people not to care what you're doing every minute. I will, that is, if I survive the bus trip with this woman talking to me about how her husband got cured of his psorosis, or psoriasis maybe, by an old revivalist preacher.

Today started out all wrong. To begin with, when I woke up, I did not remember it was the day of college entrance exams. My mother (who is sweet but very crazy) brought me hot chocolate on the painted enamel tray that she made the last time she was in the hospital. Only I was still half-dreaming— and in the dream, it was Nancy Schubert from American History class who was bringing the hot chocolate. So, right off, I had to shake loose of my disappointment about Nancy Schubert, while at the same time wondering why my mother was pulling clothes out of the closet, clothes she had decided I should wear today.

I hate it when she does things like that. So for quite a while I pretended to be asleep, listening to the empty hangers swing on the closet rod and sensing the gray September breeze as it slid across the bedcovers. Then suddenly I remembered that today was the entrance exams and I gave up pretending and went downstairs.

My father had already left for his law office, so I didn't have to act like I was looking forward to going on the bus to Springfield. My father works three days a week as the County Public Defender and has a civil law practice on the side. He is almost never home, and on those rare occasions when he is home, he is either talking to me about my future or he is looking at my mother with a curious, blurred expression, like he needs to cry, but maybe has forgotten how.

From a tired old paper bag that she has been clenching ever since she sat down, the woman on the bus offers me cinnamon candy. It seems important to her, so I take some, even though the little red hearts remind me of those Valentine presents you give to people when you are in the fourth grade. Twisting shut the neck of the paper bag, she says, "What will you do in Springfield?"

It isn't all that easy to answer her question—unless I tell her what my father believes: that I am going to Springfield High School to take the college entrance exams so I can score an early acceptance to a top-flight college. Ever since I was born, Dad has been measuring my personal progress against a standard of achievement that is as unrealistic as everything else in the town of Gretna; he doesn't seem to realize that I have already slipped through the cracks, academically speaking.

Until this very moment it had been my intention to wait out the exams at the movies, staying there in the dark certainty of the theater until time to catch the return bus at 4:15 P.M. (I have always thought it pointless to put yourself through something when you know the outcome before you've started; it's sort of like biting into a lemon.) But when I start to tell this to the woman who is sitting next to me, with her paper bag of cinnamon candy and her hairnet and her serene, expectant face, the words turn metallic and wrong in my mouth. I stare at the newspaper. It is open to the movie listings, but now the opposite page, the obituary section, catches my eye. Adopting an expression somewhere between discomfort and fear, I say, "I'm . . . going to a funeral, ma'am."

"A funeral?" she says. "Oh, dear. I am so sorry. I had no idea." Her mouth is red from eating cinnamon candy. "And here I've been running on and on about my own troubles." She shakes her head. "Well, of course. That's why you're all dressed up in a suit and tie. I wondered about the suit. Oh, I am so sorry." For a time she remains silent, as though pausing in honor of the dead. But then curiosity starts to pull at her like a dog tugging at a leash. "One of these?" she asks, pointing to the obituaries.

"Yes," I say. "That one there." And I indicate a paragraph near the top of the page. Jeanette Jarvis, it reads. I like the sound of the name.

Repeating Jeanette Jarvis over and over again to myself, while hearing the loud, consonant hum of the bus engine, I feel more in tune with the spinning earth than I have all day. So I continue. "She was my aunt on my mother's side. Mother's favorite sister," I say, knowing even as the words come out that I am breaking an important rule: Never answer a question that has not been asked.

The woman sits up straighter. "I don't exactly understand," she says. "If Jeanette Jarvis is your mother's sister, why are you traveling alone to the funeral? Where's your ma?" Her voice slants across the stale air inside the bus. Up front a baby begins to squall.

"Sick in the hospital, ma'am," I say. "And they won't tell me what's wrong with her." At this point, I turn my head away and stare out the window. Audibly I draw in some air and hold it.

"Oh, dear," she says again, softer this time. She sounds regretful of ever having started the conversation.

If I know people, I know that she will now gather up her belongings and begin walking toward the front, while the bus is yet moving, acting as if she is afraid she will miss the stop and end up traveling to the next town. She will not say another word; she will pretend it is all she can do just to get herself ready to depart the bus in Springfield. I know that's what'll happen. And, even as I know it, she is in motion.

After she leaves, I watch the city glide past the large, streaked window. You can almost not focus on anything outside the bus before it shrinks, recedes, and is gone. In one yard I see a woman wearing an apron and holding her hair against a stubborn gust of wind. Her mouth is open, and she seems to be calling to a group of children who are tree-climbing across the street. She looks a little like what I remember of my mother before she went to Willowbrook Hospital the first time: bewildered, sad.

The neighborhood yields to a series of anonymous buildings; many of these are attached to parking lots that look flat and vacant because today is Saturday. The whole downtown has a failed look to it. Signs in the windows of the stores and restaurants have been turned to the side that says, SORRY, WE'RE CLOSED. On the streets only a few people are visible; mostly I see drifters talking out loud and searching the gutters for lost coins.

Before me, like an ocean, lies an empty, disconnected Saturday that seems to hold within itself the disappointment of every human life. Even though my father is as distant now as the slow, dusty Gretna streets, the way he looks at the world from behind those tortoiseshell eyeglasses has followed me all the way to Springfield. It is my belief that he glares at the world around him because he never got out of Gretna, or into a big law firm, or anything—so he figures it is up to me now, and he doesn't want me to blow it.

The bus pulls into the Greyhound station. I sit and wait until everyone else gets off. I don't like standing behind a bunch of people while they take forever to do something really simple like get off a bus. Finally the driver looks back to where I am sitting. "End of the line," he says. His eyes watch me to see if I am going to make trouble for him.

"So soon?" I say, standing up and straightening my tie. "I must have fallen asleep." Then I pick up the newspaper that is still folded open to the obituaries. "My aunt died yesterday," I say, passing by the driver and descending into the chill, vacant, gray morning.

When I arrive at the funeral home and climb the stairs and put my hand on the silent, blank doorknob, the wind has shifted, with the fresh cold air running along beside me now like an anxious playmate, like a curious child who only wants to peek inside before running away, and the sun is encased in thick clouds. I watch the door open, yawn inward, to reveal a splendid, soundless vestibule. Then I see him standing there in the vestibule, all peaceful, nodding his head slowly up and down, without otherwise moving. "Good morning, young man," he says. "May I be of service? Who are you here to—?"

"Jeanette Jarvis," I say and sort of incline my head.

"Of course," he says. "She is in Room B. Down the corridor and to the right." He gestures slowly and smoothly, his hand sort of dissolving away. He does not appear surprised to see me; I must look older in this suit than I remember. It no longer bothers me that Mother picked out my clothes this morning, and I decide that there exists some fabulous universal design that has guided my life up the stairs and into this corridor.

As I walk, I am smelling the thick flower smell and listening to the sad, whispering respectability of the unmarred walls. Since I can remember, no one in my immediate family has died—except one set of grandparents, and they had a farm way out in Kansas. I've noticed that everybody always clams up when you start talking about death; I have been noticing that for several years.

From the corridor, while yet a distance away, I can already see the room. To the side of the doorway is a glass display case, inside which have been placed some of those black plastic letters you get in the hardware store; they spell out the name Jeanette Jarvis and the time of the funeral: 1:00 P.M. In the entrance there stands a thin woman of highboned, gaunt face and blond hair. She is watching me. "Are you the sister?" I say immediately. "Are you? What a terrible shock. I am Brady Carlyle."

Then she is at my elbow, talking to me in a hushed voice, and I answer, whispering almost. I see the open coffin. Thick curtains are drawn behind it, giving a rich, velvet feel to the near-empty room. All calm and decorous, the curtains appear to rise forever away from human frailty. Beloved Daughter and Sister is what it says on the mass of flowers that blanket the lower half of the coffin, the closed part. The body of Jeanette Jarvis is lying there as if asleep and not dead at all. Her dark blue dress seems new— perhaps she bought the dress and never had a chance to wear it. The newspaper obituary said she was for many years a Spanish teacher in the public schools and died at sixty-three. "It looks just like her," I say.

The sister murmurs into her handkerchief. "It does; it surely does. She looks peaceful, so much at rest." The sister was born Rosalind Jarvis, but her name is now Mrs. Smith because she is married to Bud Smith, the only Chevrolet dealer in Ashford, a town about two hours' drive south of Springfield—I have learned this since we met. It seems she has not seen much of Jeanette in recent years. She keeps saying how sudden the illness was, how death snatched her from their midst without warning. She gives me a little half-smile and takes hold of my arm, gripping it. "Tell me, Mr. Carlyle," she says, "how did you know my sister?"

Still gazing at the flower-draped coffin, I say, "Well, ma'am, I'm a student at Concordia Seminary is what I am. And last summer vacation, Miss Jarvis tutored me in Spanish, you see. It is my complete intention to enter the foreign missionary field next year when I graduate. That's why I must become very proficient, fluent really, in Spanish." My mind pictures craggy hillsides filled with people waiting to hear some incredibly eloquent and hopeful message from a Spanish-speaking preacher who had to travel on horseback in order to reach their village.

"Is that like going to Bible college?" she asks.

"Why, yes," I say. "Except it is called a seminary."

She looks at me, her face questioning, polite. "You look young to be graduating from Bible college."

"It's because of advanced placement," I answer and nod once with my eyes closed. When I open my eyes, I see that she is nodding, too.

Into the smooth silence she says, "When Jeanette left the church, it broke my heart. It honestly did." She looks straight ahead, talking in a remote way, as if she is saying things that need to be said again and again. "I'll never understand why she insisted on living such a reclusive life. Even as a little girl, she never let anyone get close—not friends, not her own sister. It has always seemed to me that if you live to yourself, you die by yourself. Still and yet, I wish I had tried harder to break through, to reach her."

Standing in the warm artificial light, an inadvertent witness to more than the passing of a life, I feel as if I am being carried like flotsam on the complex, intricate movement of history. Yet it seems that there is no way to go but forward. I look at the figure in the burnished coffin and say, "Well, she may have stopped going to church, but I'd say she had an incredibly strong faith."

"You would?" she says, her eyes going moist. "Oh, Mr. Carlyle, you cannot know how comforting those words are. To think that Jeanette might have come to know the Lord in her final days—it is so reassuring. And will He not leave the ninety-nine in the wilderness and go after the one which is lost until He has found it?"

"Yes, ma'am," I say. "He will." I hope she doesn't ask me to quote something from the Bible. She continues holding my arm, seeming alone and small and afraid.

Then a middle-aged man comes up out of the hush where I have not noticed him before, approaching in a manner purposeful, yet faraway. He says, "Hi. I'm Bud Smith, Rosalind's husband. Shame about Jeanette. You a neighbor?"

"Bud," Rosalind says, "you'll never guess! This is Brady Carlyle; he is a student of the Holy Scriptures, and he visited Jeanette quite often before the end." After a moment she lets go of my arm and drifts away from the two of us like she is now thinking about something else.

I turn from the coffin to look at him. He stands uneasy in the breathing aftermath of exertion, a short, fat man with blue-marble eyes set deep in his flushed and smiling face. He stands there, his ears and face red like my Uncle Joe's, looking as if he has arrived here neither by choice nor against his will, but only by the sheer momentum of circumstance. We shake hands.

The silence seems to confuse him. He clears his throat and says, "You must be the one she talked about." Not waiting for confirmation, he says, "Rosalind and I are grateful to you for being there with her. Awful hard for us to get away from the business, you know."

"Yes," I say, "I understand," adding, "It was all so very sudden."

"Yes," Bud says, "it was." He acts immensely relieved, as if these few words have the power to release him from some unnamed burden.

It occurs to me that I ought to leave now, before someone finds out that I am not a seminarian who knew Miss Jarvis in her last days. But, in that instant, I notice an elderly woman standing by the wall, her head turned, staring at me across the room. There is nothing at all in her ancient eyes: no shock, no anger, no remorse. It appears that she has been standing alone, listening maybe, ever since I arrived. She watches me, her face uplifted. It is as if there is some definite connection between us which she accepts merely as a fixed and unremarkable fact of life. She does not look at the coffin or at Bud Smith or at Rosalind; she looks at me, but without expectation, without urgency. When our eyes meet, I feel suddenly caught, drawn to her presence, as though I have been singled out for some special purpose.

"Excuse me," I say to Bud Smith, then I walk toward the ancient woman. "You must be Miss Jarvis's mother," I say. Her impassive, unrelenting eyes hold onto mine as if to a safety rope. Quietly she stands in the embrace of the room's strange eternality, her back humped with weariness and suffering. "I'm sorry," I say. "I really am. It is an absolutely terrible loss."

"Which one are you?" she says, loud.

"Would you like to sit down?" I ask, pointing to several folding chairs with leatherette seats, which have been placed in a perfect row along each wall. "I am Brady Carlyle."

"Please speak up," she says. "I'm eighty-nine years old and I don't hear worth a toot." Her slight body leans toward me; I can see where her hair has gotten quite thin, revealing the scalp underneath. I wonder if this is what my grandmother looked like—I don't remember anything about her except a hazy scent of violets.

"Brady Carlyle," I say louder.

"Oh," she says. "I don't think I know you."

"No, ma'am," I say.

"It should've been me," she says, "not Jeanette." The others in the room look hard at her, as though to quiet the intrusive sound of her voice with their disapproval. But if she notices, she does not change her tone. "I'm almost ninety. The next funeral should have been mine, not hers. It isn't natural to outlive your children; it's all wrong." She indicates the coffin with its blanket of flowers, all beautiful and serene under discreetly hidden, rose-colored spotlights. "And see there what they've done. That's not what Jeanette looks like. They've gone and made her look like someone else." The woman is close to shouting now. I can sense within her gray, frail body a tearing that is like a tearing in the fabric of the universe. Something fundamental to life has been jarred loose and is buzzing like a faulty machine part.

"I'm her mother," she says, quieting some. "Every day when she walked to school, I worried. After she left, I would stand at the window and watch until the neighborhood closed around her and she disappeared. I worried she might get lost or fall down on the playground. I worried about her crossing the street by herself. And now, you see, it's happened; I've lost her. I keep thinking she's just gone to school, and she'll be coming home again any minute. But she won't. This time she's gone for good." The loud, fluid discourse ceases. Empty of words, she stares at the coffin and at the curtains behind it as if intent upon penetrating the veil between this world and the next.

In that instant, a primitive, unanswerable emotion seizes me, and I reach into my jacket pocket for the package of cigarettes I keep there in case things get tense. Her voice hollow, abject, the mother says: "Everyone tried to talk me out of coming today. Too tiring, they all said. But Mona Jarvis isn't an invalid who can't go to her own daughter's funeral. Jeanette never treated me that way."

"I'm not surprised," I say. "Jeanette was pretty insightful." For a time I wait. But now she seems to have forgotten I am there, so I move away, edging past the leatherette chairs and the mourners, who are standing in the awkward, desolate wake of the mother's grief.

Not until I reach the corridor do I remember that I had intended to smoke a cigarette. Upon taking out the pack, however, I see coming toward me the man who waits at the entrance and directs people to the various rooms in the funeral home. "If you wish to smoke, sir, there is a lounge," he says. "It's around the corner and to the left. We also have coffee for family and guests. Won't you please help yourself?"

It seems only polite to have a cup of coffee. And I am thinking that it is still a couple of hours before the little kids clear out of the movie theaters to go home for lunch. So I make my way to the lounge, peering into each of the open rooms along the way. One room is pretty crowded compared with Jeanette's; everyone is standing around the casket of a man who appears to be no older than maybe thirty. A woman in black is wailing, sort of; it makes me feel terrible to see how young that guy was when he died.

In the small lounge a coffeepot is gurgling through the last throes of its cycle. Already there and lighting a cigarette is a man with dark-circled eyes. He sits on a sofa, which is upholstered in an odd liver-colored fabric; to each side of it are several office chairs. The room looks random, thrown together. It is completely out of harmony with the rest of the funeral home.

When I try to pour coffee into a Styrofoam cup, there is a loud hissing noise as the last stream of liquid continues flowing through the filter and onto the warmer-plate. "I hate those things," the man says, smoking.

"Me too," I say, and sit down in a chair.

He says he is Arthur Jarvis, Jeanette's brother, and I tell him my name, leaving off the part about the seminary. Next I light a cigarette, and we both smoke. For a long while the room is washed in silence; it is as though we are wrestling with a tricky scientific problem, an enigma that demands resolution.

He says, "What do you do, Brady?"

"Why, . . . I'm an attorney," I say. "Put out a shingle a little over a year ago." Visualized behind my eyes is a small office filled with law books and boxes of subpoenaed documents; across the desk from me, in the mental picture, sits a guy whose wife just died in a factory fire; he has three little kids hanging onto him.

"Is that right?" Arthur says. "You must really be some kind of whiz kid. You're so young to be out of law school."

"Advanced placement," I say, loosening my tie. "I did well on the entrance exams."

Arthur says, Is that right? a couple more times. Then he asks, "Did you do legal work for Jeanette?"

"Oh, maybe some," I say. I manage to sound as if I know what I am talking about. "Mostly it was a matter of friendly advice. It seems to me she enjoyed discussing things with people as much as anything."

"That was Jeanette, all right," Arthur says. Then he begins to look real sad; his face distorts, and he smooths his hair back in a compulsive sort of way. He leans forward, elbows on knees, and stares at the floor. "I never did say good-bye to her, Brady. By the time I arranged for the days off to come and see her, she was gone. I never got to tell her how much she meant to me."

At the moment everything I can think of to say seems ridiculous, so I remain quiet. It is hard to imagine someone you have known forever, like a member of your own family, being actually dead—gone so completely that you can't talk with them anymore, even to argue. When my mother first went to the hospital, I thought she was dead (not that I had any idea what that meant, being only five). She had a nervous breakdown, they told me, and she would be home in a few months. Only it was a couple years before she actually did get back, and by then I felt weird and lopsided, like I was meeting someone for the first time—except that she was my mother, of course.

Arthur Jarvis lights a fresh cigarette. Though he seems less sad now, he is still studying the floor. "You're lucky, Brady," he says. "Like Jeanette, you went and got yourself a good education. Now me, I never even finished high school." He says it like it doesn't matter much, like he is just making conversation. "I guess I didn't have the brains for it, so I quit."

This guy is seriously depressed, it seems to me. "Hey, Arthur," I say, "what do you mean, you didn't have the brains for it? I know lots of folks who weren't graduated from high school, and it's almost never because they haven't got the brains. What kind of business are you in anyway?" He can't be doing too badly, I figure, because he is dressed in a suit and is wearing a really decent watch. Watches tell a lot about a person.

"Oh, I worked at a dozen different jobs," he says. There is no expression to his voice. "Then about ten years ago, another guy and I bought this diner— made it into a twenty-four-hour restaurant. We're still in business, but it's a struggle from month to month."

With his face in profile, I see that his features resemble Jeanette's. Not having brothers or sisters, I am always surprised when kids from the same family look so much alike. It's amazing. These things occupy my mind a lot. "Listen, that's great," I say. "Really." I get up and offer to pour him some coffee. He accepts. "Twenty-four-hour restaurants," I say, sitting down again, "are very important to people."

"Important?" he says as if he does not understand

the word. But now I can tell he is starting to get interested in something besides the linoleum.

"Absolutely," I say. "Almost the best time I ever had was at a twenty-four-hour Mexican restaurant in Gretna—that's the town where I grew up." Arthur is looking straight at me now. His eyes are somber, as if he expects to hear some great truth. "One Christmas when my mother was in the hospital—every now and then she kind of goes off the deep end in a mental way—it was just me and my dad to celebrate Christmas. But every time I asked him what we were going to do, he said he didn't know yet and for me to wait and see."

"He wouldn't tell you how you were going to spend Christmas?" Arthur has forgotten about his cigarette. A length of ash falls unnoticed to the floor.

"Right. Not until Christmas morning. And then, just when I am figuring the day is going to be a huge failure, he says for me to put on my coat. I was pretty young at the time. I remember we walked from the apartment all the way down to Fourth Avenue. The Mexican place was the only restaurant in town that stayed open on Christmas Day. Still does, as far as I know. We ordered incredible platefuls of tacos and enchiladas. The owner gave away free dessert and kept on toasting us with Mexican beer. Dad laughed a whole lot. He ate so much hot sauce on his food that he had to keep taking off his glasses and wiping his eyes. I tell you, Arthur, without that restaurant, it would have been one miserable Christmas."

"Your dad sounds like quite a guy," Arthur says.

"Oh, he is, yes," I say. "As a matter of fact, he's a good example of what I am trying to say here." Whether or not Arthur is really hearing me, I don't know, but at least he doesn't look as depressed as he did. "You see, he didn't do all that well in school, but he kept at it. Got his law degree finally by taking night classes while he held down a day job."

"Both of you are lawyers?" Arthur says.

His question startles me a little; I didn't mean to be giving out all these private details; it's a good way to get tripped up. But then again, Arthur looks like he hasn't slept for a week, and no one else has beaten a path to the lounge to ask him how he is, so I go on with it. "Uh huh," I say. "Dad's a great lawyer. And wise, too. Before I ever went to law school, he would tell me that the main thing in life is always to give yourself to something you believe in. The rest will follow."

Then it is my turn to feel sad. When I was a little kid, my father actually did say stuff like that, no lie. But the minute I hit high school, everything changed and he began to get this terrific investment in my becoming a superior student. A little too late, if you ask me.

It doesn't seem productive to talk about my father anymore, so I say, "Tell me about your restaurant."

"Well, Brady, the restaurant's been a gamble the whole way," he says. "But I hate to give up, even though my partner keeps insisting it's a loser.

Jeanette used to say I should stick with it—now that I finally found something that made me want to get up in the morning." His shoulders hunch forward. It is as if he carries on his back the cumulative weight of every mistake and failure of his entire life. "She was probably just being agreeable because I am, or was, her kid brother."

"Jeanette, agreeable?" I say. "Not a chance." I speak in a quick and alert voice, before he has a chance to make a complete backslide into that depression of his. "She wasn't one to sugar-coat the truth."

"I suppose you're right," he says. "Jeanette never did mince words. But now she's gone. And the others"—he points vaguely toward the door—"never let me forget that I'm the only one in the family, in their acquaintance even, who didn't finish school."

"You're also the only one in the family who runs a twenty-four-hour restaurant," I say. "Where would lonely folks go on Christmas or on Thanksgiving or in the middle of the night if you didn't keep that restaurant open?"

Now, for the first time, Arthur Jarvis looks cheerful. If he were wearing tortoiseshell eyeglasses, he would bear a strong resemblance to my father.

Unfortunately, at the very moment that Arthur is looking the most like a normal human being, Rosalind pokes her head around the door and says, "There you are, Brady. I'm glad you're still here." Then her glance hits Arthur, and she frowns a little

171

(I'll bet she doesn't even know she does that), and she says, "Arthur, I do wish you wouldn't hide in here. You know, it would be polite if you came out and greeted people; it really would."

Arthur looks as if he would like to disappear off the face of creation and end up on a different, more accepting planet. "I believe I can hide in here if I decide to," he says. "If she were alive, Jeanette wouldn't care whether or not I stood around feeling foolish. Besides, my friend Brady has been saying some very important things."

If Arthur continues talking about these important ideas of mine and informs Rosalind that I am an up-and-coming young lawyer, she will get very mad, thinking as she does that I am a seminary student. And so will everyone else get mad, including me. I will be unhappy with myself for being dumb enough to believe I can keep doing stuff like this without getting seriously caught. My mouth is open to make a casual remark about the generosity of the funeral home in providing hot coffee, when Rosalind interrupts.

"The very reason I'm here is Brady," she says. "Mother wants to see him."

As it turns out, Mona Jarvis sent Rosalind because she wanted me to join the family for lunch before the funeral; she told Rosalind, who told me, that I was the only one around here who didn't consider her a useless invalid.

I go along with them, expecting every moment that Arthur and Rosalind will begin trading notes on who I have said I was. However, there is no need to get all steamed up because Rosalind does not say anything at all to Arthur until we are returning from eating lunch at one of those franchise cafeterias. As we ride along in a full-size Chevrolet that belongs to Bud's dealership, Rosalind asks from the front seat, "Have you decided yet about selling the restaurant, Arthur?"

The brother's entire body tenses. I should have gone to the movies, I am thinking, while sort of smiling at Arthur across Mona, who is sitting between us on the backseat. But instead of going to pieces and yelling or anything, he just laughs. Everyone, except me, stares at him like maybe he has lost his mind. "Hey, don't ask me, ask my lawyer," he says, nodding his head in my direction.

The remark causes the blood to rush from my face, and I spend the next minute or two peering out the car window, wondering what would happen if I were to open the door right now and sort of tumble onto the sidewalk. I keep looking out the window until at last I sense that the conversation has moved safely past the lawyer idea, and the tight feeling in my throat dissipates.

————

At exactly one o'clock the music begins. A minister from Ashford, who is known to Bud and Rosalind, has already arrived by the time we get back to the funeral home. He takes charge, talking at length with the funeral director and with Rosalind as if dealing with death and burial is no problem at all for him. The family is invited to view the body one final time, and I agree to stand with them while the coffin is being closed, although by now I am not feeling so very casual about Jeanette myself, and it would not actually harm me to be somewhere else, even back in Gretna.

The funeral director tells us where to stand (to one side, facing the head of the coffin), and the handful of folks who showed up for the service are positioned so that they are facing its length. There must be about a thousand flowers woven together in the blanket that covers the coffin. From here I can no longer read where the flowers spell out Beloved Daughter and Sister, and I'm kind of glad. I keep remembering how Mona said it isn't right that Jeanette died before she did, the daughter before the mother. It's getting clearer and clearer to me why folks avoid talking about death.

While I am understanding this, the organ music fades and the minister starts to speak; he stands at a lectern in front of the visitors, with his side to us. My throat is dry. And I feel like I was born in this suit.

All through the service I try to think about something else. Most of the time my mind drifts away without any effort at all. But so much estrangement and loss have been compressed into this place that I can't successfully block out the sadness. And in the end, I find myself watching the family as they, with full pain and fear, continue to relinquish their hold on Jeanette Jarvis. Rosalind weeps with a persistent mournfulness. Bud stares straight ahead like a man whose faith has been turned inside out. Every once in a while Mona says a word or two aloud and grips my hand. Arthur looks distracted and lost.

I don't know how we do it, but we manage to get through the funeral. Then we all ride out to the cemetery in one of those limousines with little purple flags flying from the front fenders. Hearse in the lead, our procession slips past intersection after intersection where traffic has been stopped. There seems to be an invisible barrier between us and those who wait while death passes by. Even though I never met Jeanette Jarvis and, by all reckoning, should not be here right now, nevertheless, I have been caught up by the event; I have entered the strange, unexplored region of mystery into which each of these separate, lonely people has been thrust.

When we reach the cemetery, I notice it is only the family that's there; not one of the visitors has accompanied us. Surrounded by solemn headstones, these few uncertain folks gather to offer Jeanette Jarvis back to the earth—no spectators, no organ music in the background. Overhead the clouds are heavy with rain, and from a distance I can hear the grumbling, shadowy sound of thunder. Creation itself seems burdened with the riddle of life and death.

Mona says she wants me to stand next to her. She seems more agitated now, though still she isn't crying. In Mona's voice there is nothing unusual, certainly nothing to prepare me for what happens next.

After the coffin has been positioned above the grave (artificial grass hides the yawning earth), we take our places beneath a canvas canopy. First the minister reads some prayers. Then he stoops down and picks up a clump of earth from a fresh grave nearby. It is a big clump, and he scatters fragments of it all over the coffin, including on the blanket of flowers, which has been brought from the funeral home. Then he picks up more earth and does the same thing, all the while reciting words from the Bible.

That's when Mona Jarvis releases my hand and heads for the grave. At first I think she is upset because the flowers are getting dirty. Almost immediately, however, I know she is intending to throw herself at the casket. It is as if she has realized that she must let go of Jeanette, really let go, and suddenly has found herself quite unable to do it.

I am seriously asking myself why in the world I

ever thought it was a good idea to show up at a stranger's funeral, and I am looking around for an escape route, when Mona raises her voice, making an utterly wild, uncanny outcry. Without words, she expresses a primeval rage that questions absolutely everything, and lays the questioning squarely at the feet of God.

Stunned, the others try to pull her away from Jeanette's coffin. "Please, Mother," Rosalind says over and over again, as if she is speaking to a child, or to someone who has not lived a lifetime already. Even Bud and Arthur appear to be much more concerned with the impropriety of Mona's behavior than they are with listening to her anguish. It makes me sad.

Then, before I can reflect on what I'm doing, I step between Mona and the others. "Let her scream," I say in a voice almost as loud as hers. "She's wrestling with God. Let her scream."

They all stare at me. What's more, I know I have blundered into something dark and absurd while breaking yet another cardinal rule: Don't draw attention to yourself. But I can't back down either, so I say, "I mean, that's her daughter who's about to be buried. She has a right, don't you think?"

Arthur looks calmer now, chagrined even, and he is nodding his head. But Rosalind covers her ears with her hands as if to block out both the memory of my words and the present reality of Mona's unquenched grief. She fixes her eyes on me and says, "I don't know what kind of Bible college you go to, Mr. Carlyle, but—"

Before she finishes the sentence, I am in motion. Tucking my head, I put on a burst of terrific speed and run like crazy away from the canopy and the hearse and the open-mouthed people. I do not look back. I keep on running, dodging the headstones, until at last I reach the paved road that leads out of the cemetery.

It is because I know what would have happened. In a matter of seconds Arthur would have heard what Rosalind was saying, and he would have looked at me with a hurt look because I lied to him. But if I tried to explain that I had not told anyone the exact truth . . . well, I would rather not deal with it right this minute.

When I have reached the iron gates, I keep running until I am breathing fire and can't go on. Turning then, I look back toward the cemetery. With distance the wrought-iron fence has vanished as completely as if it had been swallowed by the past. Around me are rows of simple houses with tiny front yards; I am thoroughly lost. After catching my breath, I notice that the thunder has deepened. Threads of lightning are splitting the sky; before long, the afternoon grayness will translate into pouring rain.

A kid riding a bicycle passes. "Hey," I yell, and

he skids to a stop. "How do I get to the Greyhound bus station from here?"

On the bus no one wants to sit next to me because my clothes are soaking wet. I doubt the driver would even have let me on, except that I told him I had to make it home for my best friend's wedding.

By the time we reach Gretna (and we are twenty minutes late because of a military guy who decided the bus should make an unscheduled stop at a cross-roads in the middle of nowhere), I am not in good spirits. My hair has dried in clumps; I am chilled all the way through. During the entire ride I haven't let myself think about my father, who almost certainly will be meeting the bus. Instead, I've been reading the license plates of all the cars on the road, imagining what each of the different states would be like to live in—especially if you were seventeen years old and had no visible means of support.

By this time on Saturday afternoon, Gretna's bus station resembles a downtown pool hall where only folks who have nothing else to do gather. In the midst of the station's waiting room stands my father. He looks old and sad and tired, as if he knows he is going to be disappointed before ever I say a word. The tortoiseshell glasses have slipped partway down his nose. It's a hard thing to stand in front of your father while wearing a suit that has been drenched and then partly dried with paper towels from the men's room. Especially if your father doesn't say anything, doesn't ask a single question about the college entrance exams you were supposed to take, or about the suit, or even about the state of your health.

At first I believe he is waiting for me to offer some outrageous explanation that he knows isn't true, and which will make him despair of my sanity. But then it seems that we are each weighing our innermost thoughts before saying anything, knowing that the entire future is somehow balanced on a precarious, invisible fulcrum. I am feeling a lot older than when I left Gretna this morning. I wonder if it shows in my face.

Finally Dad says, "Welcome home, son."

Which is the last thing in the world I expect him to say—so there is an extended silence during which I stand there almost mesmerized. It occurs to me that for years I have not talked seriously to him because of always anticipating some sort of criticism. But now he is simply waiting, quiet and patient, as though ready to hear whatever it is I have to say.

"Look, I don't know how to explain this," I say, "but I got caught in the rain while running away from a funeral."

After he gets through staring, he begins to laugh. He laughs so much that he has to take off the tortoiseshell glasses and wipe his eyes with a handkerchief. Maybe what I said struck him especially

funny. Or maybe it is because of the soggy condition
of my suit. Or maybe he has been saving up this
laughter for such a long time that it just came out,
and for no particular reason.

Everyone is looking at us now, and he is still
laughing. "C'mon, Dad," I say, kind of steering him
toward the door. "How about I buy you a cup of
coffee?"

Outside the bus station, we enter a fresh new
world. Rain has cleansed the town. Sun fragments
are glinting off the water droplets that cling to nearly
every surface. Even though there is almost no traffic
on the streets, we wait at the corner for the light to
change. "Dad?" I say, holding my breath in case he
has decided to get mad at me after all.

"What?" he says.

"Can we go over to that Mexican restaurant on
Fourth Avenue?"

"The Mexican place?" he says. His voice sounds
thicker than usual; he must be getting a cold or
something.

"Yeah," I say. "You know. Where we went that
one Christmas. If I remember right, they had great
coffee."

He readjusts the glasses on his nose and clears his
throat. "You have a good memory, Brady," he says.
"They do; they serve excellent coffee."

Then, walking, we make our way across the late
afternoon. Beyond our footsteps the shadows advance, always advance—expectant, eager, stretch-

ing out ahead of us toward a future as yet unshaped. The sidewalk feels solid and right beneath my almost-dry shoes, and just around the next corner is a newsstand where I can buy a copy of the Sunday *New York Times*.

18961

Lake Wales Public Library
290 Cypress Gardens Lane
Lake Wales, Fl. 33853
941-678-4004

DEMCO